Modern
Happiness

Michael Gilbert

ISBN: 0615609198
ISBN 13: 9780615609195
Library of Congress Control Number: 2012903780
Sisyphus's Joy, Monticello, IN

"If our condition were truly happy, we would not seek diversion from it in order to make ourselves happy."
—*Blaise Pascal*

DEDICATION

I would like to thank my parents, George and Judy Gilbert, for their love and guidance. There truly has been no greater gift. I am forever indebted to my siblings, Matt Gilbert and Elaine Gilbert, for their unconditional support. I extend my gratitude to Jason Lane, Don Leffler, Scot McAtee, and Brock Miller for their friendship and feedback on this novel. The author photograph is credited to my friend, Ryan Hicks. I also need to thank my friend, Chelsea Hicks, for the original cover art.

CHAPTER 1
RAINY NIGHT

Ashley Morrison

He only called when it was raining outside. I heard the phone vibrate on my bedside table. I didn't have to check; I knew it was him. It had been three years since we said good-bye. I listened to the rain patter against the window while the phone sounded again. William lay beside me, still asleep. Aram knew William and I were engaged to be married. Why did he persist in making it so difficult? The phone vibrated a third time. I picked it up as the light from the screen illuminated my face and I studied the number I had tried so hard to forget.

I didn't answer Aram's call. He knew I couldn't with William lying right next to me. That's why he did it. He was testing me. He was always testing me. I thought of the elation I felt those four years I was with Aram. His penetrating gaze is what initially attracted me to him as he stared into my eyes from across the table at the bar. A crooked smile caused me to return the favor. We talked forever that first night and when his hand gently grazed mine underneath the table, a chill ran throughout my body. Damn Aram Young. Damn the way he looked at me. Damn the way he kissed me while holding my body close to his.

I quietly arose from bed with my phone in hand. I told myself I needed a glass of water, but the true reason was gripped tightly in my palm. I walked gingerly over the hardwood floor that periodically creaked, despite my best efforts to remain silent. Once in the kitchen I poured a glass of water that I sat on the counter without taking a drink. I listened to the voicemail. His soft voice penetrated my ear. I loved the way he said my name. After the brief message was over I poured the water down the drain and sat the glass in the sink. I walked back to the bedroom and again the floor creaked underfoot. As I lifted the cover and slid underneath its warmth; William moved slightly. I kept repeating to myself that I had never been any happier.

* * *

Kiley Adams

I never tired of watching Aram sleep next to me. I loved the way his eyelashes curled upward and the way his eyes moved while he dreamt. The perfect nights were when the moonlight made his tan skin visible in the darkness. He always had one leg out of the sheets because he said it kept him cool on spring nights. The fan oscillated overhead, washing our faces with tepid air and causing his curly brown hair to remain clear of his glistening face. I slid a fingertip along his sleek shoulder. He didn't move. He always slept so soundly.

My body still ached from his presence inside me just an hour earlier. Aram's smell lingered on my skin as I leaned up to take a closer look at him. Our relationship was nearing a year, yet he had yet to reveal that he loved me. I had neglected to share that I loved him, but he knew. He had to know. God, I craved him incessantly. I had a feeling that once he figured out everything in his heart that he would propose in some perfect way. Maybe he would take me on a carriage ride in the city, or drop to one knee while we strolled down the sidewalk to our favorite diner. I wasn't sure, but I felt his heart and mine were becoming one.

Sure, I knew his ex-girlfriend had hurt him pretty badly. He rarely talked about her, but there were a few times when a sad song played on the radio and I noticed his eyes remained fixed as his mind wandered to a distant memory. Aram couldn't deny that I took care of him though. I gave him all of me. I let him have me in my car, in restaurant bathrooms, and he even took me from behind in my mom's pool a few weeks ago while the rest of my family was inside making dinner. I would do anything for him and he knew that. All I wanted in return was for him to love me and make me his forever.

* * *

Turner Brennan

Even though I hadn't heard from Aram in weeks, I couldn't get him out of my mind. It had to be after one in the morning but I remained wide awake. He told me I was only twenty-years-old and that I could not possibly understand a man ten years older. I assured him that I did. I lived for his replies to my emails. I would read them and reread them until the messages were seared into my memory. I could recite them verbatim and often would to myself late at night when my eyes were closed and I thought of him.

I still have the one letter he wrote to me two years ago when I was in the hospital. I keep it under my pillow and pull it out late at night to feel the contour of the paper that he once touched. His handwriting is barely legible but personifies his anxious intelligence. I felt his hair once and gripped it quickly before he noticed. His spiraling curls clung to my hand as he moved his head. A light sprinkling outside caused the gutters to emit a periodic tink as the droplets hit the metal.

I wondered what he was doing, what he was thinking. *Was he with someone?* Even if he was, there was no way he truly loved her.

I felt around my bedside table until I fingered the base of my lamp. I turned it on and reached under my pillow to retrieve Aram's letter. His handwriting was so urgent, yet heartfelt. I pressed my fingertip over the words, tracing the exact movements Aram undertook when composing the message. I paid particular attention to his signature. I traced it slowly before carefully folding the letter up and placing it underneath my pillow, where it belonged. The letter was perfect. He was perfect. He would be mine.

CHAPTER 2
DINNER

Kiley Adams

"What do you want, Aram? We've been together for nearly a year now, and we're still exactly where we were when we began this relationship. What do you want? Do you only want to sleep with as many women as possible? Do you ever want to settle down? Do you even care?"

Aram stared at his plate as he twisted the pasta around his fork, only to drop the noodles down on his plate without taking a bite. His disposition is what truly angered me. I couldn't get through to him. It was as if he was going through the motions. The only passionate moments we shared were associated with making love. Even then, Aram was distant. He was always so damn distant.

"So… don't you have a response?" I asked.

"To what?" he said in a monotone voice.

"Oh God, are you serious?"

"What do you want me to say?" he replied.

"Anything…"

After dinner we walked side-by-side down the sidewalk without touching. I wanted to reach for him and pull him near, but I wanted him to want it too. In fact, I wanted him to want it slightly more, though that wasn't at all appearing likely after my outburst. I was so frustrated I felt tears welling in my eyes, but I fought their release. I didn't want Aram to know how hurt I truly was. I had to be sure he cared.

I sped up my pace so that I was no longer beside Aram as we walked. He trudged along, seemingly disinterested in keeping up, which only infuriated me more. His head was down, staring at the sidewalk cracks as he walked. I moved in front of him and then stopped abruptly, causing him to run into me and reflexively grab onto my gray wool jacket. He pulled me near in an effort to steady the both of us.

"See, was that so hard?" I asked, half-jokingly. He looked perplexed for a second before he smiled. "There you go. You do have a soul."

"Of course I do. It's just dormant sometimes," he said, a little more life present in his voice than before.

"Why? What makes your soul hide?" He still held my coat in his strong grip. I turned and placed my hands on his shoulders so I could look into his eyes while awaiting a response. He smelled good. The sun shone on his face, revealing his perfect complexion. God, he was so handsome.

"To avoid being hurt, I suppose," he retorted before loosening his grip on my jacket. I tried to pull him closer, but I could feel his body go limp.

"I'm not going to hurt you, Aram. Do you believe that?" I asked, still looking into his eyes.

"How can I ever know if you will or won't?"

"You have to believe me. You have to have faith," I asserted.

"Maybe that's the problem. Maybe I don't have faith any longer."

That evening while we lay in bed I turned my head so that I could face him as he read a book. I never understood why he read so much. I guessed it was a way for him to deal with his emotions in a removed sort of way. He had never been overly expressive with me. He noticed me looking at him and turned his head. I smiled at him and winked. Aram chuckled.

"What are you doing over there?" he asked.

I brushed my hair off my face with my hand so that it covered most of my pillow. "Looking at you," I replied.

"And why is that, Miss Kiley?"

My gaze stayed fixed on him. "Because I want you. I need you. Do you need me?"

"You know I do. Just not tonight." He resumed reading after he spoke. I ran my hand gently over his shoulder, slowly making my way down his chest and to his waist. "Kiley! I thought I said, not tonight?"

"God, what's your problem?"

"I'm not feeling well," he said. *What a lie*, I thought.

"Fine! Just damn fine. I'll be here when it's convenient for you. That's what you want anyway. I was right to question you today. You really only want sex, just like every other guy, only it's always on your terms. I don't know why I thought you'd be any different." I felt a tear roll down my cheek and settle on the blue, cotton pillow case.

"Don't be that way, Kiley," he said in a flat, emotionless tone. He hadn't even noticed the tear.

"Then what is it, Aram? Is it me? Do you not want me? I don't understand," I said between sobs.

"It's just that… Oh, forget it. You wouldn't understand."

"Understand what? I want to understand. Please!" My uneven breathing steadied a bit.

"I just don't feel well. It has nothing to do with you. Nothing has changed." He took a deep breath before continuing. "I'm just working through some of my past. It doesn't matter anyway."

CHAPTER 3
DOWNTOWN

Turner Brennan

Today finally came. I had waited for three weeks and finally it arrived. I even kept a countdown of how many days remained on a silly calendar. I would never admit that to anyone, especially Aram. He agreed to meet me downtown for a gallery walk. I was so excited I only slept an hour the night before. When I awoke, it was as if the lack of sleep had no effect on me. I looked outside my window at the sun that appeared brighter than it ever had. Nature was again showing signs of life due to the onset of spring and with her rebirth, I also felt renewed. I showered with a special citrus-fragranced body wash I knew Aram would enjoy. I wanted my scent to stick to his clothing after I was long gone. Isn't that what any girl wants, to remain with her love, even when physically removed from his presence?

I felt sick when I saw him approaching me. I was seated on a bench near the courthouse and tried like hell to appear nonchalant, but I felt my stomach turning and feared that my nervous elation was somehow evident on my face. I turned my glance elsewhere for a moment, but was drawn back to him. He moved with such grace, such unabashed fluidity. I envied his confidence from a distance as he walked seamlessly toward me. I must've looked like a starstruck little girl. Aram looked down at me as the sun shone over his shoulder. I squinted as I looked up.

"Hi, Turner," he said in a cheerful voice. "How are you?"

"I'm doing well," I replied while shielding my eyes with my left hand. "How are you?"

"I feel great. I hope you're ready to explore!" I stood up after he spoke, feeling my knees weaken in his presence. *Why did I care so much? What was it about him that made me feel panicked?* "Come on, slow-poke," he playfully demanded. His three-button black blazer hugged his body perfectly with the bottom button left undone, exposing the silver belt buckle that drew my attention to his fitted dark jeans. I immediately wondered what it would be like if he ever undid them in front of me. *Would I ever know what it felt like to have him?*

A breeze chilled me enough that I buttoned my jacket as we walked down the sidewalk. "Where are we going first?" I asked, not caring in the least what Aram's response would be.

"There is no plan. I figured we'd visit a few galleries, maybe visit Sixth Avenue."

"What's on Sixth Avenue?" I couldn't help but look at him after I asked. He looked so fit walking next to me. He was so much taller than I remembered. He had to be well over six feet tall.

"My favorite diner is on Sixth Avenue. It's called Bruno's and it's amazing! You really have to try their chili dog. Half of it will be on your face by the end of the meal." Aram chuckled to himself and then turned to me and smiled.

"If you say so. I would never have expected that you would eat a messy chili dog."

"Oh yeah? I'd expect there's quite a bit you don't know about me."

"Well then, I can't wait!" I exclaimed, unsure of what to really expect.

As we studied the paintings in the galleries, I found myself drawn to observing Aram. The way he peered at the brush strokes struck me as unique. He appeared to be tracing the streaks of paint with his eyes, visually recreating the work from scratch with his mind. "Who painted these?" I asked the lady who busied herself toward the back of the gallery.

"Those are from David Adam's collection. Aren't they magnificent?" she asked as she moved closer to the canvases hanging on the wall.

"They are stunning," I replied. Aram remained transfixed by a painting of a woman weeping. *What attracted him to such sorrow?*

I waited on Aram to finish his rumination before I approached him. I didn't want to disturb his fixation. "What do you think?" I asked nervously.

"I love it," he replied simply.

"What do you love about it?" I was afraid to ask, but I had to know.

"Everything," was his only response. The more I considered it, the more I realized it was a perfect response.

I felt the warmth of the sun on my cheeks as we walked down the sidewalk amid the noise of passing traffic. I felt lighter than I had in months. Elation filled me as I noticed Aram looking at me when he thought I wasn't paying attention. *What did he want to know? How did he see me?*

"I want ice cream!"

Aram laughed at my randomness. "What?"

"I want to stop and get an ice cream cone!" I repeated.

"Uh, OK. Where did that come from?"

"I don't know, but doesn't it sound yummy?" I don't know what got into me, but Aram appeared to adore my impulsivity.

"It sounds absolutely great! Ha-ha. That's the cutest thing you've ever said." He looked away after speaking. I couldn't keep from smiling.

As strawberry ice cream dripped on my hand and ran down my wrist, I noticed Aram laughing. "What?" I asked with my mouth full.

"You're a mess!"

"Is that not allowed?" I asked, feeling a bit embarrassed.

"It's most certainly allowed. You're making my day." His voice trailed off but his eyes remain fixed on mine. It was the first time Aram looked at me that way. As I licked the side of the cone to keep the dripping to a minimum, the remainder of the ice cream dropped from the cone onto the cement. I looked down in horror. Aram couldn't stop laughing.

Aram plucked a flower from a tree and gave it to me. I gently accepted the gift and held it tightly in my hands while giving a pseudo-curtsy. Aram just smiled. "That's all you needed."

"Why do I need a flower?"

"Because you're beautiful and all beautiful girls need a flower." I felt my cheeks flush from embarrassment. "You really are. You know that, right?"

The sky took on a violet hue as the sun sank behind the tall buildings. I stood on the curb by my car making faces at Aram. "You're silly," is all he said. I didn't want the day to end, but Aram assured me he had to get back home. I didn't ask him why. I didn't want to pry. Just then he took my hand in his and pulled me off the curb. I fell into him and he caught me. He held me for a moment and then wrapped his arms around me and hugged me tightly. I hugged him back, and rested my head on his strong shoulder. He squeezed me a few times and then released me. I instantly felt colder without his body against mine. I felt so happy I wanted to cry.

"I'll talk to you soon, Turner," he said, his hands gripping my arms. I could only nod my approval. As he walked away from me, I knew I could never love another.

CHAPTER 4
CONCERT

Ashley Morrison

"What did you say?" I asked. William repeated himself. I wasn't listening though. I just nodded until his lips quit moving. He smiled as the next song started. I had been at the concert for nearly an hour and I couldn't remember one song that the band played. I remembered when my smile used to mean something. Now I feigned interest in my surroundings. I feigned emotions. I feigned life. It had to be those damn antidepressants I started taking after the breakup. *Why did Aram and I ever split anyway? Does it even matter?* The music from the band drowned out my thoughts until I found myself sitting alone staring into space. I didn't want anything. Truth be told, I felt nothing during the whole show but a gnawing emptiness.

"Would you like another drink?" William asked.

"Sure, why not?" I replied. I didn't really care. I watched William part his way through the crowd to retrieve our drinks. I loved him. I did.

William returned and handed me my rum and diet. I immediately took a sip from the small protruding red straw. It burned going down my throat and settled in my stomach, sending a rush of warmth coursing throughout my body. It marked the first discernible sensation I detected the entire night. William turned to watch the band. I remained seated at the small table. He periodically turned to look at me. I guessed he was checking to see if I was enjoying myself.

"These guys are even better in person! Don't you think?" Shana's excitement exuded as she spoke. She's William's cousin. I don't really like her.

"Yeah, I can't believe how talented they are," I said. Then I smiled. Shana grabbed my hand and squeezed it. She walked over and stood next to William. I wanted to die already.

I stirred my drink, watching the dark liquid whirl around and around in my tiny plastic cup. The ice had almost completely melted. I wondered what Aram was doing. I always wanted to go to a concert with him. He wouldn't stand across from me and watch the show. I know that. He would be standing behind me, hugging me, pulling me close while whispering in my ear. He would pull my body into his. Aram always said he wanted me closer than was humanly possible. He was always so fanatical about our love. That's what I enjoyed the most. William looked over at me. I smiled at him.

My relationship with Aram was a beautiful moment in time. That's all it was—a moment. Every moment is destined to be over eventually. Aram said he still thought of me. I wondered if that was true. I guess it truly didn't matter since I was to be married by the end of July. The wedding had become more for my mother than me. She had to have the right flowers, the right tablecloths, the right lighting, the right appetizer, and God knows what else. She cared about everything that didn't matter. I suppose everyone is that way.

I pried a cigarette from my wrinkled pack and placed it in my mouth. I dug around in my purse until I found my red lighter. I lit the cigarette and took a few drags, holding each in longer than usual and exhaling the smoke through my nostrils. My stomach felt terrible. I tried to fix my hair a bit, but that was useless too. I sat and smoked my cigarette and when it was finished I smashed the butt into the ashtray and lit another. I forgot to take my pill that morning.

Smashed cigarette butts littered the ashtray and my drink was gone by the time William looked over his shoulder at me again. He did a double take and then turned around.

"Is something wrong?" he asked.

"No. Why do you ask?"

"You're sitting here by yourself smoking a whole pack of cigarettes. I thought you liked the band?"

"I do," I replied.

"Then what's wrong?"

"Nothing." I wanted to yell that his relentless questioning was the problem. I wanted to tell him to be a man and claim me.

"Come on, something's wrong," he persisted.

"I want to go home," I said.

"Why? What's wrong, Ash?" I didn't answer him. I had nothing more to say.

CHAPTER 5
BOOKSTORE

Turner Brennan

His eyes worked busily from side to side as he scanned first one book, then a second. I watched his hands move the pages back and forth with a tenderness only Aram possessed. I wanted to make him mine right there. I wanted to promise him I'd forever cherish his presence. Oh how I desired to be someone special in his eyes. He settled on a few art books and motioned for me to follow him to the nearest table. I followed him. I would follow him anywhere, though he probably couldn't tell based on my coyness. *Could he sense my desire to please him?*

"Didn't you grab any books?" he asked. I blushed.

"No, I guess I didn't. I wasn't sure which ones to choose." That wasn't entirely true, but it was the best response I could muster with my heart in my throat. "What books did you pick?" I clumsily tried to recover as I directed my eyes toward the books he rested on the table.

"I thought you'd like this impressionist one and a collection of early surrealism. They supply a great contrast of color and imagination." I turned the impressionist book around and flipped through the pages as Aram continued. I lost track of what he was actually saying.

All I could dwell on was how good he smelled. I've never savored a scent so long. I stopped breathing a few times, just so I could experience his aroma with a fresh palate.

"So how have you been?" His question broke my trance. I noticed my heart rate increase as I struggled to respond.

"I've been okay," I paused. "How have you been?" I felt like an idiot as soon as the words left my mouth. *Why couldn't I think straight?*

"Oh, just putting up with bullshit from Kiley. I swear, I wish all women were more like you. I don't understand it. I always get involved with the wrong ones." I knew he had dated a girl named Kiley for some time, but I wasn't sure if it was an ongoing relationship. His statement suggested that he was currently involved with her. I hated her already.

"What's she been doing?" I asked. I tried to sound calm and collected, though I felt the anger welling within me.

"Typical female games. She wants to trap me. I just know it," he remarked.

"Trap you?" I pretended that I was naïve.

"Yeah, trap me. She wants a relationship and I don't want one. I mean, she's okay to hang out with, but it's seriously not going anywhere." He opened the surrealism book after he spoke and flipped through a few pages before he looked up at someone who entered the bookstore.

"That's shitty. Why is she trying to deceive you?" I felt a calming relief permeate after hearing Aram's confession. I had to choose my wording carefully. I wanted Aram to notice her flaws.

"She wants to get married. I know that's her plan. She's twenty-four years old and feels as though if she doesn't marry soon then she'll die alone and miserable. I don't understand her preoccupation with age. She acts as if she's middle-aged. It's annoying because she continually maintains that she doesn't ever want to get married, but I know that's not true. Every girl wants to get married." Aram shut the book and pushed it off to the side. His frustration became evident.

"Why are you with someone who is dishonest or would harm you?" I asked in a very innocent tone. I smiled to myself at the notion that my comments were systematically sabotaging Kiley. It served her right for harming my one and only love.

"It started off as just hanging out. I guess she started coming around more often and I didn't stop her in time. Now she's staying the night at my place and all I really want her to do is leave."

"Tell her to leave," I interjected, feeling a bit ashamed after doing so.

"I don't know. It's more complicated than that," Aram said. I didn't immediately respond. I flipped through a few pages and then closed the impressionist book. I wasn't in the mood to look at anything beautiful.

"I'm going to grab a Diet Coke. Do you want one?" Aram asked. I nodded that I did. I wasn't really thirsty but I felt a dire need for a distraction. My hands rested awkwardly on the table. If I could busy them with a drink, then maybe my anxiety wouldn't show.

I watched Aram walk away. I couldn't help it. He never knew, but my eyes remained fixed on him as he made his way to the counter and ordered the two sodas. The cashier flirted with him, but he didn't notice. Maybe he was used to people flirting with him. I wondered what it was like to have everyone wanting you.

"I'm sorry for laying all of that on you," Aram said after he returned and handed me the soda. I took a long drink from the straw to alleviate my dry mouth.

"It's completely fine. What are friends for?" I smiled after I spoke. Aram smiled back and looked into my eyes for a brief moment.

"I'm happy that I have someone I can talk to about all of this. It's been bothering me lately."

"I still don't understand why you don't just leave her. You could have anyone you want. You don't need to put up with her shit." I felt myself gaining confidence the longer I remained in Aram's company. I felt stronger than I ever had in my entire life. We weren't just conversing. We were talking about his life and he appeared to actually be listening to what I had to say.

"It's complicated," he repeated.

"As you've said."

"Just don't ever change," he said to me. I could tell from his voice inflection that he meant it.

"Change what?" I asked sincerely.

"You. Who you are. The innocence you still possess. You don't know how rare it is to meet a person that isn't damaged or jaded," his voice trailed off and I became aware that an emotion had involuntarily been exposed.

"Damaged?" I asked, searching for details. I wanted to know more.

"It's a long story," he said dismissively.

"I don't have plans," I replied. I smiled as a means to reassure him that I was safe.

"This girl hurt me years ago and I've not been the same since," he revealed.

"Who?" I asked, attempting to keep the conversation going.

"Ashley is her name. Oh forget it. I don't want to bore you with all of this."

CHAPTER 6
MOVIE

Kiley Adams

"Why don't you ever talk to me?" I asked as the previews started and the lights dimmed in the theatre. I felt the warmth of his hand gripping mine, but something was missing.

"I do talk to you," Aram whispered as he let go of my hand and stood to allow a younger couple to enter our aisle.

"You talk to me. But you don't *really* talk to me."

"What the fuck does that even mean?" he asked, noticeably agitated.

"Calm down. Never mind."

"No, you started this, so I want to know. What are you talking about?" His frustration was still evident.

"We never talk about our futures," I said in a vague manner.

"Yes we do!"

"No we don't!" My voice elevated unintentionally. "You talk about your future, but you never talk about our future. It's as if you expect that we're not going to make it. Is that what you think? Do you think that we're not going to make it? Do we not have a future together?"

"Where is this even coming from?"

"See! You're avoiding the question." I turned my head so I didn't have to look at him. I felt like crying.

"I can't believe this," he muttered.

"I can't believe you!" I exclaimed as I felt my eyes tear up.

"Are you crying?" He leaned over in order to inspect my face in the darkness.

"Leave me alone."

"Kiley... Kiley! Look at me!"

"You're drawing attention to us. Don't make a scene," I kept staring straight ahead at the screen. I feared if I blinked the tears would be released in one uncontrollable stream.

"Then look at me." I strained to keep my attention focused on the silly previews playing, but I felt myself being drawn to Aram.

"What?" I asked defiantly.

"Look at me," he repeated.

"I am." I heard my voice soften as my eyes peered into his.

"You know I care about you, don't you?" he asked.

"Do you?" I asked, feeling the first tear roll down my cheek. I looked down to avoid eye contact. Aram reached for my face with both of his hands and brought my head up so that he could look me in the eyes.

"I do. You have to know that. It's just that it's not easy for me at times to show it."

"I just..." I took a deep breath in an effort to regain my composure. "I want you to care about me as much as I care for you."

"I care," Aram restated. His hands slowly withdrew from my cheeks as I leaned into his touch in order to maximize our closeness.

"That's all I ever want," I said as another tear released. "It's all I could ever desire." Aram smiled.

"Don't worry so much, Kiley," he casually demanded.

"How can I not worry? Don't you worry?" I shuddered at the desperate tone of my voice.

"I've learned that there is no need to worry. It won't help anything. It's a useless response."

"I don't think so. It implies you care." I looked to Aram as the movie started. He didn't respond.

CHAPTER 7

MORNING WALK

Ashley Morrison

I remember when feeling came easily. I remember when art made sense. I remember when life mattered—when I believed that life had inherent meaning and that everything would work out for the better. I remembered those times as I walked along the sidewalk on my way to the farmer's market that weekend. I quit trying to talk William into coming with me. He always had an excuse. As I turned the corner onto Union Avenue, I noticed the tables all displaying the various produce. The commotion became louder as I approached. I really didn't have any reason to be there. All I do is work. Work, work, and more work is all that occupies my days any longer. I couldn't remember the last time I felt freedom in any way. Even as I walked amongst the tables of produce and watched the busied people advertising their wares, I didn't feel free. There was always some obligation that weighed on my mind. Below the surface lingered a constant anxiety that left me feeling flustered and exhausted.

"Can I help you?" some nice older woman asked.

"I'm just looking, thanks," I replied. I forced a smile and kept walking.

I stopped at a booth filled with flowers. There were individually cut flowers scattered everywhere in a chaotic mess of blooming beauty. I tapped my chin as I surveyed all the colors and shapes. I thought of a time when I would have been so inspired by the sight that I would have sketched it in the notepad I used to keep in my purse. I instinctively opened my purse and felt around, but soon realized that I had taken the notepad out a year ago when I stopped painting. I missed the old me. Painting just didn't matter any longer. Nothing seemed to matter.

"How much are the daisies?" I asked the girl working the booth. She appeared to be about my age with long brown hair pulled back into a loose ponytail. Her face was free from makeup and pretension.

"They're a dollar a piece," she politely replied.

"I'll take one, please."

"Which one would you like?" she asked in a genuine voice.

I pointed to the colorful one that caught my attention in the first place. "That one, please." She gently plucked the flower from the bunch and shook the stem in an effort to get the excess water off. The woman placed the stem on a piece of green tissue-type paper and began to wrap the base of the flower in the paper before I stopped her from doing so. "You don't have to wrap it. I'll just take the flower. I want to feel the stem when I carry it," I said. The woman smiled and handed me the flower. I paid her and thanked her. I felt her watch me as I walked away.

Preparation for my upcoming wedding felt like another rehearsed milestone void of any true meaning. William had been great, for the most part, during the last few months. He put up with my periodic whining about both of our parents and even consoled me the few times I broke down and cried for hours. It just wasn't how I imagined it. Then again, life never is, but I couldn't help but fear that it was all pointless.

I passed the tall buildings one by one as I walked home. I took time to glance at the flyers posted in the windows. There was one offering music lessons, one for classes on Buddhism, and one advertising the next street festival to take place in a few weeks. I gripped my daisy tightly and felt the firmness of the stem. The petals were full of life. It was as though flowers in full bloom offered a promise. For a brief moment, I felt my worries lift from me as I stared at the flower petals. Their hypnotizing glow allowed a warmth to emerge within me. I admired the yellow hue, the fresh scent, the smoothness of the texture. When I finally broke from my trance I was standing on the sidewalk in front of our house. I knew William would be inside waiting. I knew my life would be on the other side of that door, waiting. I took another look at the flower in my hand and suddenly felt a strong revulsion. I couldn't look at it any longer. Beauty had lost its power.

CHAPTER 8
EX-BOYFRIEND

Kiley Adams

His voice still resonated in my ear, answering the question I wish I wouldn't have asked. "A long time ago…before I met you," is what his unmoved voice echoes. It caused my stomach to turn as my heart pounded in my chest. Maybe he didn't mean it. Maybe he was only saying it to hurt me. Aram always loved to test me, to push me to the point of insanity until my pain satisfied him. I asked him the question after a heated argument over whether he would accompany me to my father's summer home on the lake for a long weekend. I shouldn't have brought it up. I know how he hates that sort of thing. He complains that he gets claustrophobic and gets panicked with obsessive thoughts that he can't escape. *Escape what? Me?* I became so incensed that I yelled, "When did you stop feeling?" I waited for his reaction. His demeanor remained unmoved by my elevated voice. He simply looked down at the floor and then slowly brought his head up again until his eyes stared directly into mine. His stoic voice never trembled in the slightest as he responded, "A long time ago… before I met you." Over and over his answer repeated in my head as I looked out the window of Ryan's apartment. Aram's words haunted me. The people below walked along the sidewalk completely oblivious. Everyone appeared so happy—everyone except me.

Ryan entered the room wearing tattered dark blue jeans that had holes in both knees and hung off his hips just enough that his striated abs became visible underneath his tight gray tank top undershirt. There wasn't any doubt that he was sexy. The man exuded confidence and sexuality, but that's all. He wasn't artistic or intellectual. He was pretty, nothing more. I looked at him and smiled. Ryan smiled back. I covered my mouth to hide the giggle that almost escaped. His presence reduced me to an immature girl again, but I had moved on. I loved Aram, but I wasn't sure if he loved me.

Ryan moved closer to the chair by the window where I was sitting. He stood over me, straddling my legs while looking down seductively at me.

"What?" I asked playfully. *Why did he always do this?*

"You know what," was his response said in a purposefully low tone.

"Don't," I pleaded.

"You visited me, remember?"

"To talk to you… I need someone to talk to."

"Let me guess, that boyfriend of yours?" he asked with an annoyed inflection.

I looked up at him as his hands began massaging my shoulders. "Yes. I don't know what to do."

"I think you know exactly what to do," he replied. His hands continued working my shoulders, his fingertips digging into my muscles, releasing the pent-up tension.

"I'm lonely," I confessed, feeling the rush of adrenaline jolt me from my subdued state.

"You don't have to be lonely, Kiley. You're here with me." He moved his right hand from my shoulder to the back of my neck. Ryan's hand gripped my neck tightly and then released me. He did it again and again until I felt my head getting heavy.

"Ryan, stop." My faint voice did little to deter him.

"I'm not sure why you love someone who doesn't appreciate you. You know I would do anything for you," he said.

"We would never work," I stated. "Remember that whole issue with you not ever wanting to get married?"

"You were always so damn conventional. Marriage is only a formality. It's a contract. Do you like contracts? Who likes contracts?"

"That's not what it represents. It represents two people sharing a life together." His hand fell from my neck.

"Kiley, are you serious? Damn, you're so naïve. You'd give up on love just to get a ring?"

"What we had wasn't love," I retorted. "It was sex."

"Great sex," he supplied. I couldn't argue. It had always been great.

"That doesn't constitute a relationship, or love. It's just sex."

"I bet he doesn't make you feel this way," he whispered. I wanted to reply that he made me feel better. Aram was the person I wanted to marry. I wanted to have his children. I wanted to be with him forever. I wanted him to be mine. Instead, I said nothing to refute Ryan's claim.

"I don't know why I'm here," I finally said in somewhat of a panic.

"Yes you do. We both know why you're here." Ryan cupped my face in his hands.

"Ryan, please..." He leaned down and kissed me. I couldn't talk. I felt his moist lips and then his tongue entered my mouth. I felt my body go limp and then I drew him near and kissed him back. "Wait... We can't do this..."

"Yes we can. No one will know," Ryan promised.

"I can't..." I repeated. He leaned down again.

CHAPTER 9
LUNCH WITH BROOKE

Ashley Morrison

"I think I'm going crazy... Maybe I've always been that way," I confessed to Brooke as we sat at the table on the patio at Frog's Bistro.

"Why do you say that?" Brooke asked chuckling. She searched my eyes in an effort to decipher if I was serious or not.

"Everything is fucked," I snapped back. "I mean, this wedding, William, all of these hours I'm putting in at the office. None of it makes sense. None of it matters."

"Honey, you're just stressed out. I think everyone feels that way on the verge of their wedding. I know I did." Brooke smiled and touched my hand with hers. I noticed her wedding band glistening in the sun and felt sick at the sight. "You'll make it. I promise."

"That's just it. I shouldn't want to only make it. This should all make me happy. Shouldn't it? I mean, is it too much to ask to be happy? Instead my mother has taken over the planning of the wedding. It's going to be some big, formal, fucking fairy tale drag of an event. I don't even want to attend and it's my fucking wedding. Can you believe that?" I took a drink from my water. A seed from the lemon at the bottom of the glass was floating on the top. I took another drink. "I'm serious. I really don't even want to go."

"Well, maybe you should talk to her."

"What's the fucking point? She already has this vision in her mind of what is supposed to happen. I wish she would consider for one moment that she hasn't even consulted me for weeks now. All I receive are nonstop texts and voicemails about what I should be doing and what is yet to be done. It's all stressing me out. I told William the other night we should just elope. He laughed. He fucking laughed. He has no clue!" I took another drink from my water. I looked away from Brooke in an attempt to keep my cool. I felt like I might just get up and leave. Maybe I should have.

"Ashley, you have to remember that this is your special day. You need a girls' night out. That would help," Brooke stated calmly as if she hadn't heard a word I had said.

"I suppose so," I replied.

"So what else is going on?" Brooke continued with such cheerfulness I couldn't stand it.

"Aram called me the other night," I said, trying to deflate Brooke's mood.

"Oh my God. Did you take his call? What did he say?" Her voice sounded both surprised and disgusted. I smiled.

"I didn't answer. He left me a voicemail though."

Brooke couldn't contain her curiosity. "What did he say?"

"He just said he missed me and wanted to see me soon. It's the same old message." It felt good to relay that information to Brooke for some strange reason.

"He never gives up, does he? I swear." Brooke's words did not match her voice inflection. She found it as appealing as I did, though she would never admit it and neither would I.

"Aram says he still loves me. He says he always will," I continued.

"What?" Brooke leaned toward me. "Do you still love him?"

"I still have feelings for him." I avoided using the word, love. "But it's over. We tried it and we failed. There's no reason to revisit the past."

"Is he with someone?" Brooke asked.

"Does it matter?" I responded.

"I suppose not." Brooke's demeanor transitioned to one of subtle despair. "I don't know why he continues to harass you. I guess you're hard to get over."

"I suppose so," I said in a flat voice. I looked out at the street as the cars drove by and wondered what Aram was doing at that moment.

"You're a lucky girl, Ashley," Brooke said assuredly.

CHAPTER 10
ENGLISH CLASS

Turner Brennan

The professor's voice droned on and on about something, I didn't know what. I quit listening twenty minutes ago. The stupid community college I attended didn't challenge me in the least. Most days it was a waste of time. I looked down at my notebook where my notes stopped after two lines and had been replaced by a page filled with sketches. I had tried to capture his eyes, but no matter how careful I tried to be, I couldn't replicate their intelligence. Aram would have thought I had lost it if he knew I spent my time on such activities, but I couldn't help it.

I felt numb when he wasn't around. My breathing became shallow and I felt uneasy. I knew he didn't think about me. That would change though. I didn't know when I would see him again. I should have made a move when we were in the bookstore. I should have at least touched his arm in such a way that would have allowed him to know that I wanted him. Maybe he knew, but I doubt it. I hate being so shy.

The sound of the dismissal bell snapped me from my pensive daze. I placed my notebook in my book bag and slung it over my shoulder. I had nothing to do the rest of the day besides shutting myself in my small apartment and thinking of when and how to contact Aram. I knew though that the likelihood of me actually emailing or texting him would be highly unlikely. I didn't want to bother him. I knew he was busy.

I stopped at some store on the corner of Ninth and Bluff that I had noticed since the beginning of term. It was some sort of eclectic art store that sold frames, beat-up props, and other miscellaneous items that anyone with a soul couldn't live without. I allowed my fingertips to graze the plastic mannequin's arm. I liked that it felt cold and looked sterile. There was a mirror leaning against one wall that distorted your reflection into some ghoulish-looking creature. I found myself smiling at all of the junk. I put a feathered fedora on and wore it for a while, just walking down each aisle with aristocratic entitlement. I ditched the hat and put on some oversized sunglasses that covered my eyes and part of my cheeks. I snapped a photo with my phone and texted it to Aram. I felt alive as I watched the message delivery confirmed on my phone.

I purchased a plastic head with four faces and a fern in a skull pot. I wasn't sure why I bought them but they made me feel happy. A slight drizzle began as I left the store and I leaned my head back to catch a few drops on my tongue. People stared at me. I just smiled and waved at them. I'm sure the skull pot tucked under my arm did little to comfort their fright. I wished Aram was with me. His presence would make the day perfect. I imagined the way his tan skin would look when wet. I had to make a move on him soon. Just then my phone vibrated in my pocket. I shifted the skull pot under my other arm in order to retrieve my phone. I looked at the phone screen and felt my pulse in my ear. It was Aram. His text said, "I love this so much." I caught a glimpse of myself in a building's window and saw I was smiling involuntarily.

I replied to Aram's text and asked when I would see him again. I arrived home before he responded. I positioned my plant on the windowsill and placed my four-faced plastic head on top of my television. It looked creepy, which is why I liked it so much. I filled a glass with water and poured half of it in the skull pot so that my fern wouldn't die as quickly as my other plants typically did. I sat the glass next to the skull pot and walked over to my bed. I turned around and fell backward onto the mattress, feeling my wet hair stick to my face as I closed my eyes. Just then my phone sounded. I reached in my jeans pocket and pulled it out to see that Aram had replied. "Soon, I hope."

I was sure he was with that Kiley. It made me sick. I didn't reply to his text. I would have to make my move soon before everything with Kiley got serious and he forgot all about me. I wasn't entirely sure how I would compete. *What did I have to offer?* I stared at my ceiling, feeling the enormity of the situation slowly smothering me. I bet he was spending the day with Kiley. Then there was the evening. She would be next to him in bed. I wished I was her.

CHAPTER 11
THE SMALLEST THINGS MATTER

Kiley Adams

I want a man who watches me walk away. I thought about that as I stared at Aram from across the table at my mother's house. Our Sunday dinners were tradition, but Aram rarely attended. I guess I nagged him long enough, or gave him enough sex that he decided he would attend for once. I didn't care what the reason was, I was just glad he was there with me. He looked at me in a casual way and I smiled at him. He looked away.

Aram drank one glass of chardonnay and then another. "Kiley, would you pour me another glass, please?" I obliged and got up from my chair to retrieve the bottle from the counter. I leaned over him to pour the wine in his glass and then gently squeezed his shoulder with my other hand. "Thank you," he said.

I thought about telling Aram that night. He probably already knew that I was in love with him, but for whatever reason, I felt compelled to tell him. I suppose I wanted to tell him so I could be sure that he knew. I never understood all of the games involved with telling someone about feelings. Aram always told me that's how people get hurt. I never understood that concept.

After dinner my mother collected our dishes and I heard the sink filling with water. I watched as she put on the long rubber gloves she wore when she washed the dishes so that her skin didn't get dry from the soap. Aram had about finished his fourth glass of wine and leaned over to whisper that he wanted another. "Do you think that's a good idea?" I asked in a hushed voice. He furrowed his brow and brushed his hand in my direction to dismiss the comment.

"Let's go to your old bedroom," Aram whispered in my ear.

"Why?" I asked, a bit confused by his request.

"You know…" He smiled.

"Oh my God, you have to be kidding!"

"Hardly," he coolly replied. "No one will notice."

"I'm not going to fuck you in my mother's house while she's downstairs washing dishes."

"Why not? What's the big deal?"

"It's disgusting and unnecessary. We had sex this morning."

"So what? I want to do it again," he said in an unfeeling manner.

"Not here," I asserted. "We can when we get home if you'd like."

Aram leaned back in his seat and finished the rest of his wine. I got up from my chair and went into the kitchen to see if my mother needed help. "That's okay," she said. "Enjoy your time with Aram. He really is cute, isn't he?"

I walked back to the table to find that Aram had filled his glass with more wine. He looked distant. It made me sad to see him drinking so much and to know that I had denied him what he wanted.

"Come on," I said while grabbing his hand.

"What?" he asked.

"Let's go to my room." I smiled at him.

"I thought you couldn't," he snapped back before taking a drink.

"Don't be that way. Come on, let's go. It might be fun," I said in a playful voice.

"That's OK."

"What do you mean, *that's OK?*"

"I mean, *that's OK*, as in I'll just sit here and drink wine. It's no big deal," he said coldly.

"Aram, don't be that way."

"What way?"

"This way… Don't act like you don't care," I pleaded. "Come on." I started to walk away from the table and turned my head to see if he was looking at me. He wasn't. Instead he reached for the bottle of wine and then sat back down and smacked his lips before taking another drink.

CHAPTER 12
MY FAVORITE COLOR

Ashley Morrison

Aram never knew my favorite color is yellow. I thought of that as I rode my bike downtown. The sun was bright but the gusting wind made me glad I had decided to wear my green military jacket. I plucked my water bottle from the dorky bag I had draped over the handle bars. I laughed as I considered how nerdy it actually looked. William constructed the silly apparatus. I've always adored it.

I peddled my bike at a moderate speed, weaving back and forth from the sidewalk to the road in order to avoid pedestrians. It made me happy to be out in the city, seeing people, but not feeling obligated to say anything to them. I hate social niceties. I stopped when I reached the bridge and walked my bike to one of the benches stationed with a perfect view overlooking the river. It appeared to be low with brown patches of land visible from my position above. I peered down at the moving water, looking closely until I saw miniature shadows of fish. I guessed they were most likely carp. The wind kicked up and rushed past my face, pushing my hair off my shoulders. I closed my eyes and welcomed its coolness.

I opened the dorky bag draped over my handlebars and gathered a bottle of water and a package of crackers I had brought for my journey. I sat on the bench and opened my package of crackers, spilling a few crumbs on my lap. I crunched the first one and thought about all of the wedding planning I was avoiding that very moment. It felt good to disappear from it all for a while. I hadn't a clue how people get married more than once. It's all so damn dreadful. My mother had been driving me crazy for months, his mother had been driving me nuts, and even William was starting to drive me insane. I kept telling myself that everything would be better after it was over, but that did little to ease the stress I currently felt.

It always seemed like I lived for the future. Aram used to say that was my biggest flaw. He said I only lived in the present when I was with him. Maybe that was true. I felt most free around him, primarily because when we were together nothing else mattered. He hated the concept of marriage and everything middle class. I did too. At least I did when I was with him. Since the breakup, I found myself reverting back to the middle class lifestyle and the subsequent promise of security. That was my problem. Everything had become too damn secure.

I bit down on another cracker and opened my water, spilling a few drops on my jeans before I took a quick drink. I loved my life. I had never been happier. William gave me what I wanted and I knew I loved him. He's a good guy with good morals. He will make a great father someday. It's just that there remained an inexplicable emptiness. I thought for years that the pervasive emptiness I felt at times was merely the remnants of the breakup manifesting in my subconscious to torment my psyche for how everything ended between Aram and me.

I used to think that the emptiness had something to do with other people and what they had done to me but as of late I had concluded that it originated from within me. I watched the people on the bridge. Couple after couple emerged. I watched a young couple walk by me smiling to each other. A middle-aged couple stopped on the other side of the bridge. They both gripped the railing as the woman pointed down at a boat in the river. People were happiest when with someone else. The thought of being by myself always scared me. Aram used to say I would never find my true self if I didn't embrace solitude, but I didn't want to be alone. Life felt lonely enough for me when I was with someone. I couldn't imagine being single. *Who would listen to my nonsense? Who would care about me? Would I even exist?* No, I couldn't think of it any longer. I wasn't sure why I still thought about Aram's insights. They were always so damn depressing. I wouldn't any longer. I felt a panicked urge to get home to William as quickly as possible. I needed to hug him and thank him for being with me. He is the person who makes me happy. William knows my favorite color is yellow. *Isn't that the way it's supposed to be?*

CHAPTER 13
HOUSE PARTY

Turner Brennan

I don't belong. It doesn't matter where I go or who I am with; I still don't belong. I parted my way through the crowded room past the groups of frat boys and sorority girls who were all drunkenly conversing while hanging on each other. A skinny drunk guy spilled some of his beer on my shirt and arm. He smiled at me and then had the audacity to grab my ass. Then a group of girls deliberately bumped into me. "Watch where you're going, bitch," the taller one said as I continued walking. I heard them laughing behind me. "Go home. No one wants you!" the brunette yelled above the commotion.

I stationed myself against the wall. *Why was I there?* I watched the couples dry-humping as the black lights caused everyone to glow. A couple next to me began making out and I tried to divert my attention when the guy's hand went up her shirt. I coughed when someone exhaled a cloud of marijuana smoke in my face. "Do you smoke?" was the question that followed from the glassy-eyed freshman. I shook my head that I didn't. "My bad," he said.

I decided if I was going to successfully endure my current setting, I would have to get drunk. I made my way to the kitchen. Two guys grabbed my ass on the way and another squeezed my right breast. I gave up swatting at them because as soon as I turned around they were already gone. When I finally made it to the kitchen, there was a long line of drunks waiting for their turn at the keg. I stood nervously at the end of the line. "Hey, you. Yeah, you..." One of the guys pouring the beers pointed to me as he yelled. "Come up here." I broke from the line and walked to the front where the guy who had yelled at me, handed me a cup full of nasty-smelling beer. "A beautiful girl like you should never wait in line." I recognized his statement as a lame come-on, but smiled and took a drink before I thanked him. "Anytime...What's your name?"

By my third beer I felt my social apprehensions dissipate and when a guy grabbed my ass, I punched his arm.

"Hey!" he said as he rubbed his bicep.

"Don't grab my ass, you fucking loser," I yelled.

"Bitch," he muttered under his breath. I didn't care. It felt good to hit the bastard. Every time a frat boy bumped into me, I intentionally spilled beer on him and then when he would recoil, I'd smile and apologize. It became an amusing game. I even found the girl who ran into me earlier in the night and stepped on her foot while she was dancing with a group of her friends. She let out a piercing scream and started to cry. I grinned as I glanced from side to side in a feigned attempt to ascertain the culprit.

I revisited the kitchen for a fourth time and didn't even hesitate to go right to the front of the line. "Hey, are you finally enjoying yourself?" the tall, skinny blond guy asked.

"I am," I declared, still smiling as I thought about stepping on that girl's foot.

"Are you ever going to tell me your name? You've reached your quota otherwise," he said as he smirked.

"What quota?"

"Your quota of beers. Unless you provide your name, I can't serve you any longer."

"What if I give you a fake name?" I asked, followed by a mischievous grin.

"You wouldn't do that."

"What makes you so sure?"

"You're not like that. There's something different about you. You're not like these other girls," he touched my upper arm innocently as he spoke.

"I think you may be correct. I hit a guy earlier," I confessed.

"Are you serious?"

"I absolutely am." I waited to see how he would respond.

"That is fucking awesome!" I giggled and covered my mouth to keep my elation as contained as possible. "Did you hurt him?"

"We can hope." He laughed and brought me close to him.

"So what's your name," he whispered in my ear.

"Turner. What's yours?"

"Ian."

"Well, Ian, I don't mean to be rude, but aren't you forgetting something?" He broke from me and appeared utterly confused. "Where's my drink?" I asked. Ian laughed and took the plastic cup from my hand and filled it. "That's better. I knew you were scared of me."

I wasn't sure whose room we were in, but I found myself making out with Ian. It felt good to be with a guy who wanted me more than I wanted him. He had to be my age or younger. His kissing was rushed and sloppy. I tried to focus on the moment but it was hard while the stench of stale beer lingered on his breath and his shaky hands tugged on my shirt in an effort to get to my breasts. "Wait," I said without explanation. "Let's slow this down."

"What's the matter?" Ian said, noticeably embarrassed but trying to justify his aggressiveness through intoxication.

"There's no need to rush anything," I stated. I didn't want my clothing removed at some trashy house party. In fact, I wasn't even sure I liked Ian. He represented a temporary distraction.

"I'm really into you," he replied lamely.

"Well, you can be into me and still respect me." He looked down like a defeated child. I took another drink from my beer and still he didn't respond. "I didn't mean it like that," I continued. "I'm just nervous."

"You can trust me," he promised.

"Can I?" I replied. *How stupid does he think I am? I don't even know his last name.*

"You can," he said softly.

We started kissing again. I kept getting drunker, even though I had stopped drinking. The room was spinning and when I closed my eyes, I found myself clutching Ian's shirt for balance. He mistook this for affection and pulled me closer. His tongue worked in and out of my mouth feverishly. I felt no connection. I merely found myself there, performing the motions, but otherwise completely removed from the actual event. I thought of Aram. I knew it would be different if I were with him. I felt Ian's hands on my ass. Then before I could stop him, his right hand slid down the front of my jeans and he started rubbing my panties with his fingers, searching for an opening.

"I think we should stop," I said as I broke from Ian's embrace. Both of us were breathing heavily.

"I don't want to. Do you?" he asked.

"I don't think I can do this," I admitted.

"You don't have to do anything you don't want to do," he whispered in my ear before softly biting my earlobe. "Come on." He casually grasped my hand in his and then directed it to his waist, and then he moved my hand lower until I felt the bulge in his pants. "Don't you want to?" he asked. I didn't say anything. Maybe I should have.

CHAPTER 14
WEDDING DRESS

Ashley Morrison

"I'm fat," I told my mother as I stared at my reflection in the floor-length mirror. "I'm too fucking fat for this dress."

"Ashely! Language!" my mother exclaimed. Betty, my mother, had been irritating me beyond belief for months and I happened to be in no mood to disguise my discontent any longer.

"Mother, it's true. Don't say otherwise." I felt tears welling in my eyes. I turned away and hurriedly shuffled to the dressing room so Betty didn't see me.

"Try this veil on while I get another dress," my mother's voice commanded from the other side of the door. *Did she even care that I felt shattered?* "We need to get an idea of what style you prefer."

I threw the veil on the floor in protest. As I slid my dress off, I looked at my chubby arms and waist. *How could I ever look beautiful on the only day that matters?* I had to work out, but I was afraid I didn't have enough time to get thinner. There's never enough time. My mother knocked indelicately on the door as she cracked it open and slid her arm inside. In her hand was another dress, this one dark blue, and she shook it with a quick jerking motion to indicate I needed to

59

retrieve it from her. I took it and hung it on the top of the door. I looked again at myself in the mirror and wiped the tear away that was slowly rolling down my cheek.

"This one isn't going to work," I yelled from behind the dressing room door with a loud but shaky voice.

"Ashley, you have to try it on," Betty yelled back.

"I can't try it on, mother, if I can't fit into it." I felt a panic attack starting.

"Ashley, you're overexaggerating. Now, we don't have many more weekends to devote to this so you have to suck it up and at least narrow the options today." I wanted to punch her in the face.

I exited the dressing room and faced the floor-length mirror without making eye contact with Betty. Immediately, as if it didn't matter, she began ruffling the dress and straightening out the fabric. I stood, stoically, like a robot who couldn't feel and allowed her to do so. "Do you like this one?" she asked.

While I changed out of the dress, I received a text from William. "My parents are visiting this weekend," it said, followed by a smiley face. I texted back a question mark, to which he responded almost immediately with, "my mother wants to work with you on the invitations." I became so incensed that I turned my phone off and threw it on top of my purse. I sat on the tiny bench and put my face in my hands. *How could William be so insensitive?* For a second I considered turning my phone on and telling him it was over: the wedding, our living together, the relationship, everything. The wedding had taken on a life of its own and in the process had begun devouring mine.

"Are you okay?" my mother's voice softly called from the other side of the door. I didn't respond. "Ashley?"

"I'm okay, mother," I said between sobs. She remained unconvinced and slowly opened the creaking door. "I said I am fine."

"Ashley, what's wrong?" she asked as she entered the dressing room. For the first time the entire day, my mother appeared to be concerned.

"Everything…" I started. I wiped the tears from my eyes with both of my hands moving from the side of my nose to the corners of my eyes. "I don't know what to do."

"I'm sorry. I shouldn't have been so insistent. You're overwhelmed. It happens to everyone during this phase of wedding planning. I should have noticed."

"It's not your fault, mom," I said in a child-like voice. "It's everything."

"Do you want to wait to do this another day?" she asked sincerely.

"What day? You were right. We're running out of time." Betty didn't say anything. "Let's just get this over with," I said.

"You should be enjoying this," my mother imparted. "This is going to be the best day of your life."

"I should be enjoying this, mother? Could you please tell me what about this whole process is supposed to be *enjoyable*?"

"You're getting married," she said simply.

"So?" I replied.

"So? It's what you want, isn't it?" I didn't respond. "Why don't you take a moment to gather yourself. I found a lighter blue dress I think you'll like. Are you willing to try on one more dress?"

"Why not?"

"There you go. That's my Ashley."

I turned my phone on again after Betty left the dressing room. William had sent a series of texts that I didn't bother to read. I only read the last one that said, "Don't worry."

I simply texted back, "Ok."

As I tried on the light blue dress my mother picked out, I thought of my immediate future. I had my in-laws visiting in two days, which would require that I clean the house and put away my pot. They would take up the entire weekend, which would mean as soon as they left I would be too exhausted to do anything else. Then the week would start and I would be back to working ten-hour days and trying to finish invitations and menus and locating accessories for a dress I had yet to purchase. At some point I would have to start working out for at least an hour at a time if I was going to tone up my arms and shoulders, which would be bared in virtually any dress. I felt sick. I didn't want to do any of it. I wanted to give up. I wanted to disappear. I looked at myself in the mirror. My cheeks were swollen and my eyes were red from crying. My shoulders slumped forward and my arms jiggled when I moved. I felt like a wreck and somehow I had to open the door of the dressing room and pretend that everything was all right. As I readied myself to do so, I took one last look at myself in the mirror and said aloud, "This is life."

CHAPTER 15
ARAM VISITS

Turner Brennan

His presence did little to deter my melancholy. "I've been sad lately," I confessed while looking down at my bare feet. I was seated on the edge of my bed while Aram sat in my only chair, facing me. My small apartment didn't provide much room for company. I twirled my brown hair as I awaited Aram's response. My frayed jeans tickled my heels when I moved them across the wooden floor.

"Why have you been sad?" Aram's eyes remained hidden behind his sunglasses.

"I'm not entirely sure," I said, still feeling the ill-effects of my hangover lingering. "I haven't figured it out."

"There's nothing for you to be sad about. You're young, talented, and beautiful." I blushed briefly. "You need to remember that."

"You're too kind, Aram." It felt strange to talk to him in such a conversational tone. "I'm sure it's just a funk. I'm not worried about it. It's just that sometimes I wonder if there's any point."

"Any point to what?" he asked.

"Any point to life. Does life just consist of a series of random events? And if so, is there any meaning?" I asked in a rhetorical manner.

"You're thinking way too much, Turner."

"I suppose so."

"What the hell is that?" Aram asked while pointing to the plastic head with four faces situated on my television.

"It's my fun purchase from the thrift store."

"It's hideous," he stated bluntly.

"I know. That's why I like it," I said, feeling my mood lighten.

"I like it too. It's perfect," Aram said while staring at the head and smiling.

I stood from my position on the bed and walked over to the window. "Did you notice this?" I asked while pointing to my skull pot. The fern had already started leaning toward the sun. I thoroughly enjoyed the premise. "You should go there with me sometime," I claimed before I had an opportunity to consider any doubt about the boldness of the request.

"I should," he stated. My stomach turned with excitement. "Let's go get a coffee," Aram said after looking at me for an extended moment. I figured he was sizing me up in some manner, but I wasn't sure.

"Sure!" I slid on my slip-on canvas shoes. Aram stood and led the way. I stopped to shut my door and lock it before turning around to find Aram looking at me in the same way he did when I stood by the window to show him the skull pot. "What is it?"

"I prefer you like this," he said.

"Like what?"

"I prefer you happy."

I held my paper cup, feeling the heat from the coffee against the palm of my hands. I wanted to tell Aram that the source of my sadness had been the distance between us. I wanted him to know that he had the ability to assure that I would be happy forever. All he had to do was allow me to show him how much I loved him. There was no possible way he had ever been loved as much as I was capable of loving him. I was sure of that. Still, for whatever reason, I felt compelled to keep my feelings to myself. I worried that if I said too much, he would leave and I would never hear from him again. I always feared that he'd disappear one day and I'd be in a state of eternal sorrow. I had to have him. I just had to.

"Why are you so quiet?" Aram asked while eyeing me as I looked pensively out my window at nothing.

"I'm sorry," I said. "I guess I just have a lot on my mind," I said nonchalantly.

"Like what?" he asked. His persistence made it difficult to conceal my emotions.

"Nothing you'd be interested in," I said, followed by a feigned chuckle that I emitted anxiously.

By the time Aram sat next to me on my bed to look at some sketches I had completed the other day on campus while waiting for class to start, the coffee had started to make my stomach feel uneasy. I felt perspiration on my forehead. When I turned the page, my fingertip stuck to the paper. Despite my aching stomach, I felt an emotional comfort that I rarely felt when in the presence of other people.

"This is my favorite," Aram said while pointing to the sketch of a couple sitting in the grass while kissing one another. "You make it appear as though true love is possible."

Right when he said that, something compelled me to act. I wasn't sure what inside me snapped, but before further deliberation, I leaned over and kissed Aram's lips tenderly. My initial movement was a bit rushed, but when our lips touched, I regained my confidence and allowed my lips to go limp just enough that I could feel his lips grip mine for an instance. Then he broke from me.

"Turner..." Aram began as he leaned back in an effort to regain his composure.

"I'm sorry," I responded instinctively.

"No... It's just..." Aram proved unable to complete a thought. I looked down at my trembling hands and then back to Aram. My eyes remained fixed on him as I waited for him to speak.

"Turner, it's just that you're so young…" he continued. "We can't do this," he finished.

"I'm not too young, Aram. I'm sorry, I thought you wanted it too." My voice cracked when I spoke.

"It's not that I don't want it. It's just…"

"What?" I interrupted, feeling the urgency of the issue weighing on me.

"You're innocent. See this?" he said pointing to his favorite sketch of the couple seated in the grass. "See this? This is what I mean. You're innocent and happy and that's the way you should always be. I love that you're that way and I'm not going to do anything to diminish any of those qualities."

"How could you do anything to diminish those qualities?" I asked. His logic made no sense to me.

"I'm not like you. I've been hurt and I'm not over it. It's corrupted me in some way. It's caused me to lose the capacity to feel. At least it seems as though that's what has happened. Either way, I'm not going to be responsible for corrupting you as well."

"You won't," I assured.

"You can't say that, Turner. You don't know what I'm capable of."

"Aram, you know I like you," I confessed awkwardly.

"We can't do this. You're too young," he repeated.

"Don't say that. You're going to make me cry."

"That's exactly what I'm talking about. I don't want to harm you," he said while looking directly into my eyes.

"You could never harm me," I replied, fighting back my tears.

"You don't know that, Turner," he said, still staring at me. "Don't you see?" he asked, followed by a pause. "*I* don't know that I wouldn't harm you," he continued as his eyes unfocused and his gaze became empty.

CHAPTER 16
ANNIVERSARY

Kiley Adams

I could barely contain my excitement. I moved from the oven where the bread baked at a low temperature to the stove where I mixed the pasta in the boiling water. I had almost browned the sausage and had since set about stirring Aram's favorite spicy marinara sauce in the pan, watching it bubble between stirs. Aram would be home any moment and I couldn't wait to surprise him with his favorite dinner. When I found out I would get the afternoon off work, I decided to make him a special dinner to celebrate our one-year anniversary.

Aram opened the front door and shuffled to the bedroom. It must have taken him a moment to smell the food. "Kiley, is that what I think it is?" he asked.

"Your favorite," I yelled back, smiling to myself.

"You sweetheart," he yelled in a louder voice. I heard his footsteps getting nearer as I rushed to drain the pasta and prepare the plates on the table next to the ornately arranged dinner placement. "What is all of this for?" he asked.

"Go ahead and get your plate. I have to get the bread out of the oven. You can start by getting your pasta," I said as I slid the oven mitt on and reached in the oven to retrieve the browned bread. "Do you want wine with dinner?" I asked nonchalantly.

"Do we have any?"

"I picked some up earlier. It's in the refrigerator if you'd like to grab it," I offered. Aram just stared at me smiling as I placed the pan holding the bread on the stove top. "Use these tongs to get the bread," I said as I held the pan up to show him what I was referring to. "The bread will still be very warm."

As Aram prepared his plate, I dimmed the lights in our modest dining room and lit the candles I placed in the center of the table. I could sense Aram's surprise as he entered the room and placed his full plate on the table. I smiled at him before grabbing my plate and heading to the kitchen. I didn't get too much pasta and I only took one piece of bread. I needed to lose eight pounds and had decided to start my diet two days ago.

I watched the flickering light shine off Aram's face while he ate. The shadows only accentuated his already tanned skin. He looked so attractive in candlelight. I wondered if he ever looked at me with the same fascination.

"This is wonderful," he commented with his mouth half full.

"I'm glad you like it."

"You didn't have to do this. But I'm glad that you did." He looked up at me, his eyes shining through the darkness.

"I had hoped it would make you happy," I said in a soft voice. I took a bite. I didn't feel hungry.

After Aram had finished, I quietly arose from my seat and took his plate to the kitchen while he poured himself another glass of wine. "Kiley, you're the best," he said as I walked away.

When I returned, I sat across from Aram as he sipped his wine. I stared at him until he noticed. "What?" he asked as a smile crept over his face.

"Thank you," I said simply.

"For what?"

"For this, for being you, for everything," I replied.

"I'm not following," he remarked.

"This is exactly where I want to be. I'm with you, cooking for you, looking at you, and later I will give myself to you. It's perfect. I can't imagine a better life."

"Wow... I don't... I don't know what to say."

"You don't have to say anything," I told him.

"I'm sorry we haven't been getting along lately. I don't know what it is," he said.

"Don't be sorry. It doesn't matter. All that matters is now and us being together." Aram's face appeared serene. "We'll make it," I said in a hushed, yet confident voice.

Aram didn't say anything. Eventually he looked up from his glass of wine. "Do you think so?"

CHAPTER 17

A WALK IN THE PARK

Ashley Morrison

I shouldn't have come. There was a sickening feeling in the pit of my stomach as I sat on the bench facing the fountain. I watched the water shooting upwards only to cascade back down into the pool of water. I shouldn't' have come. I decided to give him another ten minutes, even though my watch indicated he had twenty minutes before we were supposed to meet. I felt panicked and decided I needed to leave soon. I shouldn't have agreed to meet Aram.

Aram arrived early. Just as I gathered my purse and prepared to leave the park, I noticed him walking along the sidewalk. His whole disposition shifted when he noticed me. I stood to hide my anxiety as he approached.

"Ash, oh my God, how are you? I haven't seen you in so long," he said, his voice shaky. He reached to hug me. I hugged him back, partly because I didn't know what else to do. Aram felt familiar and oddly comfortable to me as he squeezed my body against his.

"Hello, Aram. It's nice to see you." As the words came out of my mouth, I suddenly realized that I meant what I had just said. It marked the first sentiment I had expressed in weeks that was genuine.

"Look at you. I mean…Look at you!" Aram said as he released his grip and looked me up and down. "You look so great!" he exclaimed. I felt my face flush from embarrassment.

"Thank you. You look good too," I said. "I mean it." I hadn't meant to say the last part. It came out without warning.

"Do you want to sit here, or walk?" Aram asked while still staring at me and smiling.

"I don't care," I said. "I guess I'd prefer to walk," I stated after considering the options.

"Sounds perfect to me."

As we walked, Aram playfully bumped his shoulder into mine just enough to throw me off course. "Stop it," I demanded. I really enjoyed it though and regretted my outburst once he stopped. We didn't say anything for the longest time. I found myself getting lost merely walking beside Aram. I couldn't even accurately describe my surroundings. It all felt dreamy. I noticed he would periodically turn to look at me. I pretended as though I didn't notice, but every time he did, I felt butterflies in my stomach. A dragonfly landed next to the sprinkler as we approached and somehow everything felt right.

"Are you really going to go through with it?" Aram asked out of nowhere.

It took me a minute to fully register the question. "Go through with what?

"You know what," he said as he looked at me. His disposition suddenly became very serious. "Are you seriously going to make me say it?" I then understood he was referring to my engagement to William, but I didn't want to be the one to acknowledge it. An awkward silence followed. "Are you really going to marry that guy?"

"If you mean William, then yes," I answered defiantly.

"I can't believe you," he snapped back immediately.

"Why?" I felt my confidence almost instantaneously dissipate when confronted by Aram.

"You have the audacity to ask, why? Why? Because you love me, that's why," he said in a forceful voice. "Or did you conveniently forget that?"

"Aram, don't…"

"Don't what?" he interrupted.

"Don't do this."

"Why? You're about to *marry* someone else. Am I supposed to accept that the woman I love is going to marry another guy?"

"I love him," I said.

"Then why don't you look in my eyes when you say the words? You may be able to lie to yourself, but you can't lie to me… not about this." I stopped walking and turned to face Aram. I looked directly into his eyes. I couldn't speak.

"See? I told you. Why don't you give me another chance? I'm not denying our relationship had problems before, but we can improve."

"It was dysfunctional," I interjected. I felt better after speaking.

"I'm not saying it wasn't. We were young. We made mistakes. But can't we try again? It's obvious we love each other."

"I'm not in love with you," I replied.

"Yes you are," he stated.

"Don't tell me how I feel. You don't know. You haven't been around."

"I know you."

"No you don't!" I almost shouted. I looked away and started walking in an effort to calm myself before I screamed or cried, whichever came first.

"This is what you always do," he said while trying to catch up to me.

"What? What the fuck do I always do?" I shouted. I stopped walking again. I didn't care if I was yelling. I couldn't contain my frustration.

"You always run away. If life gets too stressful, or you don't want to actually solve a problem, you just run away. You're a quitter."

"I don't know why I agreed to meet you," I said. Anger allowed me to keep from crying.

"You know exactly why you agreed to meet me. It's because you still love me."

"Would you fucking stop? Just stop!"

"You're upset because it's true."

"Aram, you have a fucking girlfriend. How can you talk this way? Does she know you still have feelings for me? What would she think about that?"

"This isn't about her. This is about you and me. This is about us."

"There is not an us!" I screamed. "Quit saying shit like that. You sound stupid. You're delusional. You have a girlfriend. I have a fiancé. Whatever we had is over. That's all there is. Quit trying to say there's something still lingering. You're only making this tougher on both of us." I felt a tear escape my left eye and run down my nose. I didn't bother to wipe it away. I didn't care that Aram saw it. He needed to see the harm he was inflicting on me.

"That's all bullshit. I don't have a girlfriend. I have a distraction. You have a fiancé because you believe you're supposed to get married."

"You're a mean person. You hurt people. How could you say that your live-in girlfriend is a distraction? That's just mean."

"Maybe I'm just more honest than you are. If you truly love William, let me ask you this..." He paused. "Are you enjoying the wedding preparation? Is this wedding really for *you*, or is it for everyone else?" He looked into my eyes after he spoke the words. "Ash, you know that no matter what happened in the past, I've always wanted you and I always will. I'll always love you," he said in a collected voice.

"I can't do this now, Aram. I just can't." Another tear rolled from my eye along the side of my nose.

"We're running out of time," Aram said while maintaining his focus.

"It's over," I said coldly.

"Not if you still love me," he retorted.

"I have to go."

"Think about it, Ashley. Please, if you ever cared for me, at least think about what I've said. If you love William more than you love me, then you should marry him. If you don't, then maybe you need to rethink all of this."

"I have to go." I turned and parted from Aram as he stood in the middle of the sidewalk toward the entrance of the park. There he stood, still awaiting my response. As I walked away, I felt his eyes follow me. It was over.

CHAPTER 18
A TEXT AT MIDNIGHT

Turner Brennan

Everything changed the first of May. Just after midnight my phone vibrated on my nightstand. I had class early the next morning. When I rolled over to see the illuminated screen casting its light toward my ceiling, I considered ignoring it. As soon as I picked my phone up and squinted to see the message my heart stopped. It was Aram. "Are you awake?" was the message. It was quickly followed by, "Are you busy?" I lied and replied that I was awake. "Can I come over?" came back the reply in less than a minute. When I asked if he meant now, he quickly responded, "Yes…please?"

I agreed to see Aram. He said he'd be over in fifteen minutes which barely gave me enough time to brush my tangled brown hair and put on an old pair of frayed jeans with holes in the knees and a vintage Doors t-shirt that was just tight enough to highlight my bra-less breasts. When the knock sounded I froze, feeling my breathing stop. It really was Aram Young.

He hugged me as soon as he entered my apartment. Immediately I smelled alcohol on him. His appeared unkempt, which was the only time I could remember seeing him when he didn't look absolutely perfect.

"I'm sorry for this." He verbalized his apology as he walked past me. He stood by my bed.

"Don't be," I said, wanting nothing other than to care for him. I could tell he needed it. "What happened?"

"Do you have anything to drink?" he asked, ignoring my question.

"Yes. I have…" He interrupted me before I could finish.

"Anything with alcohol will do," he blurted. His t-shirt clung to his muscular chest and shoulders. When he moved, I could see the flatness of his stomach. Even when Aram was a mess, he was sexy.

"Let me get you a glass." I walked into my kitchen and opened a bottle of red wine from France my mother purchased for me. I had kept it for two years and planned to open it for my twenty-first birthday, but I didn't tell Aram. I opened it as casually as one might open a cheap bottle of cooking wine. I filled a glass for Aram and poured one for myself. I then approached Aram carefully, making sure to steady myself so I didn't spill any of the expensive wine. He smiled when I handed him the glass. He sat on the edge of my bed and I sat in my chair. Then Aram took a long drink, followed by a sigh of relief. "So what happened?" I repeated.

"She's getting married," Aram said while staring into my eyes. "She's actually going through with it!" He stared at me for another long moment before looking away. Then he took another drink from his wine. His glass was already almost empty. I sipped from mine, feeling the potency almost immediately as my stomach warmed. I felt the tension in my shoulders gradually lift.

"Who? Are you talking about Ashley?" I asked, feeling stupid after doing so.

"Yes. Ashley." He finished his drink and stared at the glass for a moment before sitting it on the floor beside his foot. "I don't know why, but I'm upset about it."

"Did you talk to her today?" I asked, still feeling completely lost.

"Yes. I met her in the park. You should've seen her. She still loves me." His voice drifted a bit as his eyes looked past me.

"She told you she loves you?"

"She didn't have to. I can tell. I know her better than anyone." His eyes returned to mine. I took another drink from my glass. "I just don't understand how she can go through with it."

I didn't know how to respond. Aram's eyes glazed over as he became lost in his thoughts. I stood from my seat and picked up his glass. I refilled it in the kitchen and returned. He only noticed I had done so when I extended the glass to him. He nodded his appreciation and took a drink. I did the same and felt an upsurge of confidence.

I sat beside Aram on the edge of my bed. He didn't move. "I'm sorry," I said softly. "I don't know what else to say. I don't understand it either, Aram." He took another drink and then turned to find my eyes fixed on him.

"Thank you. I'm glad I came to see you," he finally imparted while still looking into my eyes. He took another drink from his glass and sat it on the floor. I still held mine, but didn't feel the need to drink any more. I already felt semidrunk.

I could have never predicted what happened next. Aram leaned into me and as his lips made contact with mine, I felt his hand on my right breast. His grip felt firm, yet gentle. My lips parted and his tongue entered my mouth. Our tongues touched lightly at first, and then with more force. I submitted to his will. I felt his other hand reach behind my head and grab a handful of my hair. He pulled my head back by my hair just enough that an involuntary gasp escaped. Our kissing became passionate and I felt the fabric of my t-shirt rubbing against my erect nipples as Aram's hand moved over one and then the other.

"I want to please you. I want to make you feel good," I told Aram in a drunken whisper. He smiled back at me. "I'll do anything you want." Aram let go of my hair and I leaned in and kissed his lips, this time sliding my tongue in his mouth and briefly becoming the aggressor. I felt the muscles of his abs as he leaned back on my bed. I moved my hand lower and felt his jeans, which were loose on him even though he wore a belt. I tugged on the belt lightly and then moved my hand lower until I felt all of him. "I want to please you," I repeated. Aram didn't say anything.

Aram tasted better than any guy I had ever been with. I couldn't take all of him, but as I worked up and down I felt his hips sway with my movements. Both of his hands caressed my hair. It took every ounce of concentration to give him my best. His moving became more exaggerated and I could hear his breathing become uneven. My hand was wet from my own saliva. I felt a pulsing. As he climaxed he pushed my head down and held it there until the moment was over.

CHAPTER 19
FROM AFAR

Kiley Adams

Aram still wasn't home. I decided to go downtown and get some fresh flowers for the apartment since Aram never wanted to go to the market with me. The sun shone overhead as I strolled down the sidewalk. Two young guys stopped after they walked past me. I noticed them looking at my ass. "Do you have a man?" one of them yelled. I smiled as I turned around but didn't say anything.

I bought the bundle of fresh flowers from an older woman who called me sweetie. I held them next to my body as I walked so that the petals would be protected until I could place them safely in my car. As I turned the corner from Fifth Street onto Salisbury, my heart stopped beating. It was Aram. He was sitting outside a café drinking coffee from a white paper cup while conversing with a girl. I didn't recognize her. I stood, transfixed. *Who was she?* She appeared to be younger than me. Her hair was a similar color to mine, though it was longer and straight. The girl's skin appeared tan. I wondered if she was from here. *How did Aram know her?*

I remained motionless for I don't know how long before I snapped out of my trance and left in the direction I came before Aram noticed my presence. Aram smiled when he looked at her between drinks. My mind raced. I told myself not to worry. I had to remain rational. She may have been an old friend. Maybe she was someone he knew and just happened to bump into. The more I considered the options, the more it didn't make sense. He hadn't answered my texts earlier. He had been away longer than he said he would. Maybe I was being suspicious, or maybe I was being too naïve.

I kept telling myself what I saw represented something entirely harmless. I repeated to myself that Aram was innocent. I only saw him drinking coffee. *Is anyone ever innocent?* I walked for two hours considering the possibilities before I returned to my car. By the time I returned home, the flowers I had purchased had already begun to wilt. I tossed them into the trash. I felt a nervous energy coursing through me. I paced, poured a glass of water, poured the water down the drain after one drink, folded a few towels from the dryer, and then I turned on the television only to turn it off a few minutes later.

Did Aram know? Did he know about Ryan? Oh God, if he did, he'd never forgive me. I couldn't hide my guilt well. Maybe Aram picked up on it. Maybe he wanted revenge. I deserved it. I deserved to be freaking out. Maybe he wanted me to find him. Maybe that's why he didn't respond to my texts. Maybe it all was an orchestrated game. I had begun to think all life was only a game.

Aram entered the apartment casually, as if nothing had happened. Maybe nothing *did* happen. I didn't immediately go to greet him. My heart pounded in my chest. I felt my hands getting sweaty. I had to calm myself. Aram would sense something was wrong. "Kiley..." Aram called from the bedroom. I attempted to settle myself. I felt sick.

"Did you have a good day, beautiful?" Aram asked as he unbuttoned his shirt and flung it on the bed.

"It was okay," I said, feeling the lump in my throat prohibiting a lengthy response.

"Is something wrong?" he asked. I stopped breathing.

"No, why?"

"Just curious. You sound upset or tired."

"I guess I am a bit tired," I replied.

"I'm sorry."

"You're in a good mood," I blurted, unable to refrain.

"I suppose I am," he coolly stated. "Should I not be?"

"No, I'm glad you're happy." I felt a rage burning deep within me, but maintained my calm on the surface.

"Do you want to watch a movie after dinner?" he asked.

"Sure." I wanted to shout at him, tell him I knew, but I didn't. I needed him. I would do anything for him. I had to become better for him.

CHAPTER 20
COFFEE WITH ARAM

Turner Brennan

I hadn't seen Aram since I went down on him the other night when he spontaneously visited me after his meeting with his ex. I couldn't even bring myself to say her name. That evening represented the first time I ever witnessed Aram lose control. As he approached where I stood on the corner of First and Harrison, I noticed he had recovered as I expected. His shoulders were pulled back as he confidently strolled down the sidewalk to greet me. Aram wore an untucked, white button-down shirt with a gray cardigan over it. His jeans were a dark blue and perfectly covered the top portion of his reflective black boots he wore in casual settings. His appearance intimidated me. I bit my lower lip when he spoke.

"Hey, Turner. How are you today? You look absolutely lovely." Charisma oozed from him, blanketing me with a false-confidence I only felt when in his presence.

"I'm doing fine, sir. How are you?" I asked, feeling foolish for some reason.

"I'm doing great, and quit being so formal." Aram pulled me into his body and hugged me tightly right after he spoke. I scrambled awkwardly to hug him back. I became embarrassed when my arm became trapped against him momentarily. Aram didn't appear to notice.

"Shall we get some coffee?" he asked while gesturing with his hand that I should lead the way. I started walking to the café. I looked back to see Aram following me.

After we each had a paper cup full of steaming coffee, Aram led us to a table on the patio. We each sat in the metal chairs that were positioned around a small table. Aram scooted his chair to the side so that he could watch the traffic on Main Street. I did the same and we both sat silently, gazing at the passing cars as if that's exactly where we belonged—with each other. A young boy dropped his fruit smoothie on the ground and began to cry loudly. The mother attempted to console him but his wails became increasingly disturbing. Aram never wavered. It's as if the cries from the distressed child had no impact on him.

"I suppose I should address what happened," he said in a soft, inconspicuous tone. He took a sip from his coffee.

"You don't have to explain anything," I replied, surprisingly with a hint of conviction.

"No, I should. It's unfair to you that I showed up the way I did."

"It wasn't at all unfair. I agreed to see you," I said in his defense.

"Still…Please let me explain."

"Okay," I conceded.

"It's just that I don't understand how women can be so cold. Ashley loves me but is marrying another guy and it doesn't make a damn bit of sense to me. Either way, I was upset and didn't know where to go…"

"You know I'm always here for you," I interrupted.

"I know. And thank you for that. But, I shouldn't have shown up that drunk and that upset. It won't happen again."

"I really don't mind," I insisted. A long pause followed. Aram took a drink from his coffee, followed by a second. I took a drink from my plastic cup and felt the tepid liquid settle in my stomach, causing my anxiety to worsen. We purposefully avoided eye contact.

"Are you sure everything is okay?" he asked in a hesitant tone.

"Yes, why do you ask?"

"I mean, after everything that happened the last time I saw you... I just want to make sure you're okay."

"I'm fine. Don't worry so much. I told you I wanted to please you. I only wish I would've been better," I disclosed inadvertently.

"Better? You were great," he claimed. I knew he only said it to make me feel better about myself. I was sure he had been with prettier, more experienced girls. In fact, that's all I had thought about since. I dwelled on the notion that he had been with girls better than me. I suppose everyone wants to be someone else.

"I appreciate that," I calmly replied. "I don't regret anything. I'd do it all over again."

"That's just it..." he began before stopping.

"What?" I felt my stomach twisting as I awaited his response.

"I fucked up."

"How so?" I asked, barely able to breathe.

"You know I have a girlfriend. I cheated on Kiley."

"I won't tell anyone," I promised.

"I appreciate that, Turner. I really do. But what we did can't happen again. It just can't." I felt the whole mood change. *Was that why he asked me to coffee? Was this all a ploy to ensure his alibi remained intact?*

"I understand," I conveyed in a flat tone.

"Don't hate me, Turner," he pleaded. I didn't hate him. How could I? I knew he had to say it would never happen again and I also knew that he needed me to agree to that principle, but I knew the spark between us the other night had ignited something. He could repeat over and over that it couldn't happen again and I would agree every single time, but deep down, I would never believe it.

CHAPTER 21
SAD AFTERNOON

Ashley Morrison

I stood barefooted in an old pair of jeans and an old green concert shirt I don't remember ever buying, watching the rain patter against the windowpane. I viewed the rain as a distant observer, some way removed from the external world just enough that none of it felt real. My cellphone vibrated in my front pocket and broke me from my distracted stupor. I viewed the screen. It was Aram. I thought about tucking it back into my pocket and trying to forget. But William was gone and truthfully I was lonely. I answered on the fourth ring.

"Hello," I said, as if I was unsure who it was.

"Hey, Ash. How are you?" Aram's soothing voice said into my ear.

"What do you want?" I snapped, perhaps too intentionally to be taken seriously.

"Whoa, calm down. I want to talk to you."

"About what? What could we possibly have to talk about?" I wasn't sure where my animosity was coming from, but it surfaced unconsciously.

"Everything," he said simply.

After my initial outburst I settled down and spoke to Aram in a civilized tone. "I'm sorry for snapping," I imparted. "It's just that everything has been so stressful. Still, that's no excuse to take it out on you."

"Don't worry, Ash. I know it's been tough for you. I didn't call to start anything or to make matters worse for you. I called to tell you that I care about you..."

"Aram, don't."

"Hear me out." He paused to ensure I would allow him to finish. "I care about you and because of that, I want you to be happy. I realize last time I saw you that I may have neglected to properly impart that to you. I want to apologize if that was indeed the case and assure you that I do care for you and always will," his voice sounded even and sincere.

"I really appreciate that," I said, swallowing afterward in an effort to ease the lump forming in my throat.

"You deserve to be happy."

"I just..." I felt my eyes watering and tried to hold my tears back before I remembered that I was alone in the house. Tears simultaneously rolled down my cheeks from both eyes. "I just feel so alone," I finally muttered in between sobs which I could no longer conceal.

"Ash, don't cry."

"I can't help it."

"Why do you feel alone?" he asked. A long pause ensued before I mustered the composure to respond.

"We're all alone, it's just that I can't cope with that reality. I hate it. There's no real companionship between people. It's all a farce."

"Where is this coming from?" he asked, obvious concern present in his voice.

"I don't belong. I just want to disappear. Then all of this wouldn't matter any longer. Then I wouldn't matter any longer."

"Don't say things like that," he demanded in a stern voice. "You're just overwhelmed. You know you get this way when you're stressed out."

"I know, but this is different. This is everlasting. I feel it weighing on me."

"It's not forever."

"Isn't it?" I asked. "Isn't it forever?"

"Only if you want it to be," he replied. "Is that what you want?"

"I don't know any longer. I don't want anything anymore. I feel empty inside."

"You're not empty inside. Before you blew up on me in the park, I saw you smile."

"It wasn't real," I said defiantly.

"Ash, remember who you're talking to. It's me. That smile on your face in the park was real. I know the difference between your real smiles and your forced ones. The one in the park was unmistakably real." I thought back and considered what Aram said. I think he was right.

"I don't know what to do."

"You have to follow your heart," Aram stated calmly.

"What if I don't have one any longer?"

"You have a heart, Ashley."

"I don't know if I do."

"You know I'm always here for you. No matter what. You know that, right?"

"I do and I appreciate it more than you could ever know. I hope you know that I am here for you too," I said the last part without thinking and wished I hadn't. "It's just that everything has changed."

"It doesn't matter. I'll always be here if you need me," Aram said.

"I know. I really do. You may be the only one."

"Can I see you again?" he asked.

"I don't know..."

"Think about it. I'd like to see you soon, just to talk."

"We'll have to see."

I hung up the phone and pushed it back into my front pocket. After doing so, I wiped the tears from my eyes and slowly calmed my breathing. As I looked out into the gray sky and heard the rain hitting the window, I thought about what I had told Aram. It was true. I did feel alone. I did feel empty. I didn't have a heart any longer. I remembered when that premise alone would have caused me to descend into a deep despair. What scared me most of all was that I wasn't despondent over the notion. It had become my reality. I couldn't feel any longer.

CHAPTER 22
WHO IS SHE?

Kiley Adams

I awoke around nine in the morning and sat up in bed. I watched Aram sleep for I don't know how long. He always slept so peacefully. His back was facing me and the blanket had slid down enough to expose his bare shoulder. I tenderly touched his skin. My fingertips traced the contour of his shoulder socket before I stopped in order not to wake him. I tugged the blanket over his shoulder so that he wouldn't get chilled. I decided to cook him biscuits and gravy. I knew he would love it.

I stood over the sausage cracking and popping in the pan as the aroma from the gravy filled the kitchen. Aram remained asleep in the bedroom. All that I could think about was my age. Twenty-four and going on twenty-five sounded so damn dreadful to me that I intentionally attempted to distract myself from dwelling on it. No matter how hard I tried, I couldn't quite abandon my preoccupation: *I may never get married.*

Aram emerged from the bedroom wearing nothing but black boxer briefs that accentuated his tone body nicely. He must have slipped them on after waking because he always slept naked.

"Did you sleep well, darling?" I asked while providing the final touches on the sausage gravy and biscuits before preparing his plate.

"I did," he said while rubbing his eyes with both hands. "Did you?" he mumbled in a barely audible voice.

"I slept soundly and actually woke up before my alarm!"

"I noticed," he replied in an apathetic tone. "What's for lunch?" Aram asked the question as he made his way past me, expecting that I would fix his plate.

After I had placed Aram's plate in front of him, I made my own and joined him at the table. I watched Aram as he ate and waited for him to say something. He never did.

"Would you like to go downtown later today? Maybe we could get a cup of coffee and do some exploring," I said in an innocent tone. I examined Aram carefully, trying to detect even the slightest bit of guilt or hesitancy. He remained unmoved.

"What would we explore?" he asked, his voice void of emotion.

"I don't know. That's why it would be exploring. We could walk around and do whatever. There wouldn't be any plan."

"We'll see," he replied. I could feel the anger intensifying as I watched him lift his fork to his mouth.

"Who is she?" I asked. I couldn't take it any longer. The charade had to end.

"Excuse me?" Aram said. He took a drink from his milk before lifting his eyes to meet mine.

"You heard me, Aram," I said in a curt tone. "Who is she?"

Aram shifted in his seat before responding. "I have absolutely no idea what you're talking about, Kiley, but this is obviously one of your schemes to start an argument for God knows what reason and I'm not getting sucked into it!" His aggravation sounded rehearsed.

"I saw you," I screamed. "I fucking saw you, so don't sit there and deny it to my face!"

"You saw what, Kiley? What do you think you saw?"

"Don't act like I'm stupid or paranoid. I saw you with her."

"Who?"

"That's what I'm asking you! I saw you with her at the café. So what, you will get coffee with a girl you won't even name but not with your girlfriend who cooks for you, cleans for you... does everything for you? Is that what you're telling me?" I waited for Aram to respond. Instead he merely stared at me and then started eating again as if I hadn't spoken. "Don't ignore me, damn it!"

"What do you want me to say?" he yelled back.

"How about the fucking truth, for once? That would be a great start!"

"She's an old friend I happened to bump into. We had coffee, Kiley. Is that not allowed? Am I not allowed to drink coffee with anyone but you? Do you know how fucking ridiculous that sounds? You're losing it." He glared at me.

"I'm not losing it..." An involuntary sob interrupted my speech. I felt my mouth getting dry as I looked for any noticeable emotion in Aram. I knew he could sense the pain in my expression. "I just want you to be honest," I finally mustered.

"I am honest," he claimed immediately.

"Then why didn't you... Why didn't you tell me about her?"

"What's to tell?" he said blankly. "Should I tell you every little detail that happens in my life? Doesn't that sound a bit absurd to you?"

"I don't know what to do."

"I don't know what you should do either," he stated calmly.

Aram ignored me after I questioned him about the girl. I had no way of ever being certain if Aram told me the truth or not. His answers seemed viable, but I still possessed a strange feeling that something wasn't right. When I entered the living room, I found Aram lying on the couch, still wearing only his boxer briefs. As I studied him I couldn't maintain my anger. His tan skin appeared perfectly smooth. His disheveled curly hair made him look even sexier than when it was styled. As he lay there, I couldn't help but find myself inexplicably drawn to him. I wanted him. I loved him.

"I'm sorry," I said as I stood in the doorway, leaning my shoulder against the doorframe. Aram didn't look up at me. "Aram, don't be angry. I love you. I'm sorry I get crazy sometimes." He moved his head so he could look at me. "Please forgive me."

"Kiley, do you believe me?" he asked.

"Yes," I said, still unsure.

"That's all I want."

"I believe you," I reiterated.

"Come here," he commanded while holding his arms out toward me. I didn't say anything as I approached him. I couldn't.

In the bedroom there remained no indication that just thirty minutes ago Aram and I had fought. Aram kissed me with passion. He undressed me quickly, almost tearing my shorts in the process. I didn't care. My mouth met his again as I wrapped both of my arms around his neck. He lifted me onto the bed. I wanted him. He wanted me. I held him tight to my body as I kissed his lips.

As he moved on top of me I whispered, "Take me." I kissed his lips again before he broke from my embrace to answer.

"Roll over." I looked into his eyes as he stared down at me. Turning over, I felt him grip my hips roughly and enter my body. His strokes were deep and forceful. It felt so good. He pulled my head back by my hair and bit my right ear. "Damn, you feel good, Kiley." I tried to respond but my head was pulled so far back that my voice was impaired due to the tightness in my throat.

As soon as Aram finished I collapsed on the bed. As I lay on my chest I heard Aram's footsteps leaving the bedroom and entering the bathroom. He turned the faucet on and I heard him washing his hands. While I awaited his return, an overwhelming fear struck me. I had forgotten to take my pill that morning.

CHAPTER 23
APOLOGY

Turner Brennan

"Don't hate me," I began after meeting Aram outside my apartment. "Please, don't hate me."

"What do you mean?" he asked while looking directly at me.

"I don't know. I just don't want you to hate me," I repeated, finding myself unable to articulate my emotions with any more clarity.

"Turner, I don't hate you. How could I? You're the sweetest girl I know," he said in a soft voice as he reached for my hand, squeezing it in his before letting go. "You know that, right?"

"I don't know what I know," I mumbled while looking down at my shoes.

"Let's go up to your apartment," he said abruptly, possibly because he wanted to avoid making a scene. I agreed to and led him up the stairs to my second-floor apartment.

As soon as I walked through the door and turned to face him, a deluge of memories swarmed my mind as I thought of the last time we were together in my apartment. I thought of how he looked sitting on my bed, how his lips tasted of bitter wine, and how he tasted when I went down on him. It all appeared in my mind as a rehearsed fantasy. I admired him as I waited for him to speak. I wanted him again.

"We should talk about this," he began.

"I'm sorry for even bringing it up. It's stupid, I know."

"It's not stupid, Turner. It's important that you feel comfortable enough to talk to me."

"I do," I interjected.

"Good," he stated simply. "That's what I want." A long pause followed as Aram searched for a way to begin what he intended to say.

"You know I care for you, right? You know that don't you, Turner?" Aram asked.

"Yes, I know you care," I said, unsure if he really did.

"I think the world of you. You're young, attractive, intelligent, and a great artist." As Aram spoke, I cringed. Beginning with compliments meant he would invariably provide something he deemed I would find potentially distressing. I couldn't take the suspense.

"Thank you," I said calmly, in spite of my inner anxiety.

"It's true. However..." There it was. The moment when everything would end and I would be reduced to juvenile ruminations over what could have been. Suddenly I felt the urge to shout out in order to interrupt whatever he was about to say. I would not lose him without a fight. "...as you know I'm in a relationship with Kiley."

"I know," I said, fighting the urge to impart I didn't give a fuck.

"It's just that we can't do this. I can't put you in the middle of this shit. It's not fair to you," he said. I recognized the traditional male reversal and it repulsed me that Aram apparently thought so little of me that he actually thought the maneuver would work.

"I'm kind of already in the middle," I said to thwart his ruse.

"That's just it. I don't want to make things any worse than what they already are."

"She doesn't know, Aram. Unless you told her, there's no way she knows," I stated confidently.

"She doesn't know everything, but she knows something," he said.

"How?" I felt it necessary to call his bluff.

"She saw us," he confided.

"Where?" I felt a surge of adrenaline.

"She saw us at the café. Don't worry, I told her you were a friend and she bought it. It's just that I can tell she's still a bit suspicious." He looked at me with a concerned expression.

"I don't care if she knows, Aram." I said in an expressionless voice that sounded distantly foreign, even to me. "I care about you and I don't care who knows."

"I care about you too," he said in an obvious attempt to console.

"So what's the problem?" I could see Aram tensing as he shifted his weight from one leg to another and back again.

"The problem is we can't continue this. I don't want anyone hurt." I wanted to scream at Aram that he was witnessing me dying right in front of him if he would quit being so self-involved for a few seconds and pay attention.

"So you do hate me?" I wanted Aram to internalize the concept that perhaps his behavior did indicate an element of malice.

"No I don't!" he exclaimed. "I told you I don't."

"It sure feels like you do. It feels like you want to abandon me."

"You're not understanding…"

"No…you're not understanding!" I shouted, unable to contain my passion any longer. "You're doing exactly what you say you don't want to do. You're hurting me. I'm being punished for caring about you." Tears streamed from my eyes and rolled down my cheeks before dropping to the floor.

"That was never my intention."

"I can't help caring for you," I said between sobs. "I just can't!"

"I need you to care for me," Aram said while bringing me close to him and holding me tightly against his body. "I just have to protect you."

"From what," I said in a barely audible voice.

"From me," he said.

"I can't stop caring…"

"I'm not asking you to. I want you to care about me. I care about you."

As Aram stood in my apartment holding me in his arms, I questioned why he considered himself so dangerous. I didn't want to believe he could cause any irreparable harm. I closed my eyes and allowed my head to rest against his muscular chest. His arms remained wrapped around me in a comforting embrace. I believed Aram when he said he cared about me. I had to.

CHAPTER 24
WHAT DO I DO?

Kiley Adams

Ryan stared back at me blankly as I sat cross-legged on the floor in front of him. "What do I do?" I asked again.

"I don't know what to tell you, Kiley," he said in his usual, indifferent tone.

"Goddamn it, Ryan. Can't you do better than that?" My hysterical crying became momentarily tempered by my frustration.

"He doesn't care as much as you do," he stated in the same flat tone. "There are only two possible responses for you. You can either break up with him, or you can accept that you care more than he does and deal with it."

"Deal with it? That's your answer?"

"It's not my answer. It's *the* answer if you choose to stay with him. That's the problem with you women. You think you can change us. You think if you throw pussy at us that we'll somehow transform into some perfect guy you've always wanted. Let me clue you in, Kiley. That never happens. It's a fucking fantasy, nothing more." I shuddered after he spoke. I realized later I did so because there remained the potential that perhaps he was right.

A numbing sensation came over me as I stared at Ryan. He sat on his sofa wearing a white, form-fitting, long-sleeve t-shirt and old blue jeans. His hair was tousled to make it appear as though he was not entirely obsessed with his looks. Of course he looked hot, but the problem was he knew it. I could tell he knew he was sexy based on the way he looked at me when I spoke. His arrogance remained present at all times. What really turned me on about Ryan was his simplicity. Nothing about Ryan was complex. He was a gorgeous idiot. Perhaps that made him the perfect guy.

"Let's get out of here," Ryan said. "Do you want to get some coffee or something?"

I sniffled. "Sure," I said.

"You probably want to wash your face, don't you?" He asked in a tone that implied that I should.

"Yes, thank you." I replied, feeling as though I had to.

"I'll get you a washcloth."

Ryan took me to some obscure coffee shop on the east side of town. He thought he was being discreet, but I knew why. He didn't want to be seen with me. He was probably fucking a bunch of different girls, and in his feeble mind he figured this would ensure that he wouldn't be discovered as the womanizer he truly was. What he didn't know was, I didn't care. Guys like Ryan will never really settle down. I knew that and it didn't bother me. He didn't talk much and was pleasant to look at.

"When did you start drinking cappuccino?" Ryan asked as we sat down. "I thought you only drank straight-black coffee."

"I suppose I've changed," I replied. My answer appeared to confuse Ryan momentarily before he dismissed my comment entirely.

As we sat outside sipping our coffee our dialogue reached a standstill. The silence didn't bother me. I watched the people walking by. A slight breeze caused the tree branches to sway. I noticed the clouds moving ever so slightly and thought about how I used to lay in the grass at my mother's house when I was young and watch the clouds for hours. An involuntary smile emerged as I considered the memory of those simpler times. I almost forgot Ryan was there at all until he spoke.

"What are you doing over there?" he asked.

"Just thinking."

"Thinking about what?"

"Easier times." Ryan's disinterest became evident. It didn't offend me though. The moment was all mine.

Back at his apartment Ryan offered me a cigarette. "I quit smoking," I said proudly.

"What? Why?"

"Aram didn't like it."

"Oh, for God's sake, Kiley. You're turning into someone entirely different because of this guy."

"Maybe I like the new me," I said.

"Maybe you don't," he stated. "Maybe I don't."

"Luckily, we're not together anymore, Ryan, so I don't have to try to impress you," I said in a bitchy tone.

"You shouldn't try to impress anyone. But, hey, whatever."

I grabbed Ryan's cigarette from his mouth after he lit it and took a drag. I blew the smoke in his face. "Happy now?"

"Does it matter?" he asked blankly.

CHAPTER 25
MOMENT OF WEAKNESS

Ashley Morrison

Life oscillates between meaning and an inexplicable absence. I had come to believe that premise over the past few years when everything ceased making sense and my life became some sort of blurry existence that resembled a dream. I couldn't keep trying to care. It hurt too much. I had reached my limit and I suppose that's when I started imagining life as a series of rather arbitrary events that lacked any inherent meaning. That way of thinking should have bothered me, but it didn't.

Aram arrived at two in the afternoon. I opened the door and smiled as I looked at him standing on the porch, his hair wet from the downpour and his gray, short-sleeve, pearl-snap shirt blotted with dark water spots. As he entered the house, I smelled his scent which caused my heart to beat faster. "Do you have a towel," he asked while taking off his shirt. "A hanger would be nice too so I don't have to wear this goddamn soaked shirt." I didn't answer. I watched him remove his shirt. His abs strained as he withdrew one arm from a sleeve and then the other. He had been tanning. He appeared darker than he used to be when he was with me. I became conscious of my pulse. Aram looked so good to me.

"Sure, let me get you a towel," I said calmly.

"And the hanger?" he screamed to me as I disappeared down the hallway.

"OK," I shouted back.

When I returned, I found Aram standing by the entranceway shirtless, looking at a photo of me with William. I froze where I stood and watched Aram. He stared at the photograph. Aram then lifted the antique wooden frame from the oak side table by the entranceway.

"What are you doing?" I interrupted.

"Nothing," he replied while continuing to study the picture. "You're not happy here," he said.

"I'm smiling aren't I?" There was a long pause as he continued staring at the picture.

"It's not genuine," he said candidly.

"Aram, stop..." I pleaded.

"It's an empty expression. You appear to be smiling, but you're removed from the moment. You're not really there. Only someone who truly knows you would be able to discern the difference between your real smile and a fake one like this."

"You don't know anything," I retorted.

"I recognize it. It's how I look when I'm with Kiley."

"Don't say her name," I commanded.

"Why not? I'm not engaged to her."

"Why are you doing this?"

He looked up from the photograph and stared directly at me. "Because it's true and you know it," he whispered without blinking.

Everything felt familiar. His touch, his scent, his breath; everything was just as it used to be, only better. When Aram kissed my neck, I felt the tip of his tongue on my skin. I couldn't take it. I kissed him once, twice, and a third time before he pushed me onto my bed. I wasn't sure how we ever got to my bedroom as I looked up at Aram, who stood over me eyeing me with such lust that I had no idea what to expect. We had made love hundreds of times in the past, if not thousands, but this was different for some reason. There was urgency in every look, every touch, and every movement. Time was running out for us.

"Take me," I whispered in Aram's ear as he lowered himself on top of me. I kissed his chest as he did so and then his neck. My hands gripped the sides of his face as I pulled his mouth to mine. I kissed him deeply, feeling his tongue perfectly massaging mine. I couldn't take it. I wrapped my arms around his neck and spread my legs. My mind remained blank. All I wanted was Aram.

We lay next to one another panting, our bodies glistening with sweat as we struggled to regain our sanity. I combed my hair back with my right hand before my arm collapsed on the mattress. I could hear Aram breathing beside me. My forearm touched his. His skin felt warm and moist. I wanted to taste him again. I turned my head so that I could see him. When I did, I found him already looking at me. He smiled at me. I smiled back. I didn't know what I was going to do.

After I took a shower with Aram and started to get dressed, I thought about what had actually just happened. "Aram," I shouted from the bathroom. "You can't tell anyone what just happened. You know that, right?"

"Of course," he replied in a jovial tone.

"I'm serious."

"I know you are."

"Listen," I said as I exited the bathroom to find Aram almost entirely dressed. "This shouldn't have happened. I'm sorry if you feel as though I'm leading you on. I'm not. At least that's not my intention. It's just…" My tears came unexpectedly. I escaped to the bathroom without finishing my thought.

"Ash, you can trust me," he said, his voice getting closer to me. I shut the door. "Ashley, don't be this way," he pleaded. I turned the faucet on and splashed cold water on my face. After I dabbed my skin dry with my towel, I caught a glimpse of my reflection in the mirror. *Who had I become?*

I finally opened the bathroom door. Almost immediately upon doing so, Aram started in. "Ash, are you okay?"

"Aram, please just listen to me," I said, feeling my voice trembling again. "I need you to seriously not say a word. This shouldn't have happened. God, what's wrong with me?"

"Nothing is wrong with you, Ash. There's something we share that could never be understood by anybody else. Whatever *it* is, we have it."

"Aram, just stop. There's no *it*. I've been a wreck lately. I've been a fucked-up mess. This is my pattern. I self-destruct. I sabotage anything that's positive in my life."

"Ash, don't fucking dismiss what we have."

"We don't have anything any longer…"

"Then what the fuck just happened? You weren't saying that twenty minutes ago. What is wrong with you? Why do you insist on denying what we have."

"Fucking stop!" I screamed. "You're making this worse." My hands were shaking. I walked to the window, partly to make sure William was still gone, and partly because I couldn't look at Aram.

"I won't say anything to anyone," Aram said in a stoic tone. "I promise."

I took a deep breath and turned to face him. "Aram, I don't mean to get so upset at you. You don't deserve it. This isn't your problem. This wasn't your fault; it was mine. It's just… I don't know what to do any longer." I stopped talking because I feared I would start crying again.

"Don't worry, Ash. I would never hurt you. I've done that enough in the past." I smiled. I wasn't sure if I meant to or not. "You need to take some time for yourself."

"That's not possible," I snapped.

"Well, that's what you need," he insisted.

"I'll be OK. I just need to grow up."

"It's overrated," Aram said. He smiled at me.

"It's necessary."

I walked Aram to the door and gave him a hug. As I felt him pulling me into his body I told myself that we would not meet again. That was it. It had to be the end of everything between us. Of course, I didn't tell him that. But it was over. It had been over for quite some time but I had been afraid to let go. Maybe I had been afraid my entire life. I wasn't certain. But I was sure that I could never see Aram again.

"You know, Ash…" he stopped midsentence. "I don't know how to say this," he said while standing on the porch.

"You don't have to say it, Aram."

"But I want to. I think I need to," he said in a pained voice.

"No you don't. There is nothing left to say."

"Ash…" he paused. "OK." He walked a few paces and then turned around slowly to face me once more. "I'll always…"

"Don't," I interrupted.

"You don't want to hear the truth?"

CHAPTER 26
MIDAFTERNOON WALK

Turner Brennan

I decided not to go to class as I stood in front of Larimer Building on campus. I felt too anxious to sit in the auditorium and listen quietly to the professor drone on in a monotonous voice. I couldn't bear it. I had too much on my mind. I couldn't stop thinking about Aram and the last talk we had in which he revealed that he had the potential to hurt me and that in order not to, we had to remain platonic friends. I knew he had to say that to me. I also knew I had to pretend to understand. Pretending didn't come easily any longer though and I wondered if Aram found it equally difficult.

The bookstore on First and Hampshire provided the necessary distraction. As I walked down the aisles I smiled to myself. I remembered how excited Aram had been when he picked out art books and then showed me his favorite paintings. I thought about how happy he had been that day and how when he walked away, I couldn't stop staring at him. That day marked the transition. Aram knew I loved him and from that moment forth, any indication that I didn't became a mere formality forced upon us by Aram's circumstance.

I sat on the patio and sipped my soda from the long red straw protruding from the Styrofoam cup. Clusters of people filed by me. No one made eye contact. It made me appreciate how lonely the world can be and how no matter what, I would forever be unknown to anyone but myself. *Why did I love Aram so much? What made him so unique?* My soda tasted flat and watered down so I stopped drinking it. I watched the ice cubes glistening in the sunlight and wondered if everything beautiful would eventually cease to exist. *Would my love for Aram remain forever?* I had to have faith that it would. I stared at my cup, watching the ice shift ever so slowly as it melted in the sun's warmth. Then, without thought, I stood up and walked away.

I hadn't planned to stop by his place. It sort of just happened. I walked downtown for a while but nothing helped. I dropped by the art store, but even the wacky items in there did little to diminish my festering angst. I had to see where he lived. I had to witness his other life. I had to quell the obsessive thoughts that kept me awake at night. I needed to confront the possibility of seeing Kiley. A gnawing pain in my stomach reminded me how much I hated her. I knew it was entirely irrational to hate someone I had never met. But I hated her. I truly did. She committed the only sin I could never forgive. She took Aram for granted.

I only knew the address, nothing more. Aram mentioned it in an email and probably forgot he had done so. As I approached 713 Elston Drive, I became aware that all of my preconceived notions about the place proved incorrect. He lived in an average apartment building complete with weathered, white paint on the siding that made the property appear depreciated. I don't know why, but I stood outside the building for a few minutes staring upward because I knew he lived on the second floor. I realized my doing so was foolish. I couldn't help it. I wanted to know more about him. I wanted to know the real Aram Young.

As I walked away from Aram's apartment building I saw his old truck parked along the street. I stopped. I wanted to walk right up to it and place the palm of my hand on the hood in an attempt to gauge how long he had been home. I didn't though. Luckily my inhibitions kicked in and prohibited me from perpetuating my foolishness. To my knowledge, no one had noticed my presence. Not that it would matter if they did. No one knew about my relationship with Aram.

I could feel Aram's presence. I questioned whether he ever felt mine. I left feeling even more unfulfilled than I had felt when I decided I had to see his place with my own two eyes. My anxiety had not been relinquished by the venture. My obsessive thoughts instead morphed into questions concerning Kiley. *What did she look like? Was she there with Aram? If so, what were they doing? Did she ever say she loved him? Did he ever tell her he loved her? Does anyone even know what love is?* When I finally arrived at my apartment, I dropped my book bag on the floor as I walked toward my bed. I collapsed on top of the comforter and stared at the plain-white ceiling. I felt a few tears escape from the corners of my eyes. They trailed down the side of my face and tickled my earlobe. I hoped all of my worrying would prove worthwhile. *God, why did life have to be so difficult for some, and not for others?* My preoccupation had shifted from Aram to Kiley. *Was she prettier than me? Did she kiss Aram better than I did? Did she give him better head? Did she fulfill him in a way I never could?* No matter how hard I tried, I couldn't stop dwelling on those notions. My stomach turned. I felt hot and then cold. Everything in my being begged me to stop caring, but I couldn't. I couldn't help but consider that perhaps I would never be good enough for Aram.

CHAPTER 27
SHOPPING FOR A PUPPY

Kiley Adams

"Aram, what about this one? Isn't it so cute?" Aram only rolled his eyes as I pressed my finger against the glass to indicate which one I was talking about. "Oh come on. Don't be that way."

"Why are we here?" he asked in a solemn tone.

"Because I want a puppy," I replied in a playful voice.

"We don't need one."

"I didn't say we did," I said. "I want one!" I tugged on Aram's arm but he didn't budge. "Why are you in a bad mood?"

"Kiley, have you thought about this at all? Have you at all considered what getting a puppy entails?" His eyes stared directly into mine.

"It's not a car, Aram. It's a puppy. And yes, I've considered that it will be work. I'm not a child."

"It's going to chew up everything in the apartment. Not to mention, it'll have piss and shit everywhere."

"I'm not a child," I repeated.

"You're behaving like one."

"You don't have to be hurtful. There's absolutely no need for that." I turned and walked away from him.

Aram followed me. I wasn't sure if he did so out of concern or because he had nothing else to do. I never could read him. I looked at a few more dogs but none of them caught my eye the way the black lab did. I returned to the lab and smiled at it through the glass cage. He wagged his tail from side to side and emitted a muffled bark between pants. "Can I see this one?" I asked the employee who happened to be nearby stocking the shelf with canned food.

"Let me get the key. I'll be back in a minute," the young girl stated.

"OK," I said impatiently. I turned to find Aram behind me. "What?" I asked defensively.

"Kiley, would you goddamn consider what you're doing for one second? We don't need a dog. I don't care if you want one or not."

"I don't know why you're being so fucking mean to me," I said in a hushed voice in an effort to avoid creating a commotion in the store.

"Someone has to be the voice of reason."

"I swear, you have no love in that heart of yours. Not one fucking ounce." I trailed off when I noticed the employee returning with the key. "Never mind," I said to the employee as she held the key in her right hand. "We're going to wait. Maybe we'll be back." I had a terrible feeling that we wouldn't be back.

I stormed out of the store with Aram following a distance behind me. I walked quickly but he didn't attempt to catch up. I stopped near a bench where I began to cry. I kept my back to Aram in an effort to shield my face from him. He eventually caught up and stood next to me.

"What's wrong? Do you want the damn dog that bad?" he asked.

"It's not the dog," I said between sobs.

"Then what is it?"

"It's you," I revealed. "It's you, Aram."

"That doesn't make sense. You're not making any sense."

"I'm making perfect sense if you cared to pay attention."

"How is that so?" The way he asked the question made me think he really didn't know.

"Are you seriously that clueless?"

"What?"

"Why don't you want a dog, Aram? Forget those fucking excuses you gave in the store. What's the *real* reason. No bullshit!"

"I already told you…"

"Oh, for God's sake," I interrupted.

"What the hell is the matter with you?"

"It's not the dog you're avoiding," I said in a stern voice. "It's commitment. You're afraid to commit to anything, especially me."

"What the…"

"Don't act that naïve, Aram. You know it's true. You're afraid if I get a dog it will inconvenience you. You're always so goddamn concerned about being inconvenienced. You're inconvenienced by any commitment that requires you to give a little of yourself. God forbid we share something. God forbid we try to be a normal couple."

"We are a normal couple, aren't we?" He asked the question as if he truly wanted me to supply an answer.

"We are anything but normal. You know what I worry about?" I asked.

"What?"

"Do you really want to know, or do you not care? If you don't care, let's just go home and forget this day ever happened."

"What do you worry about?" he asked in a patronizing voice.

"I fear that no matter what I do, it will never be enough for you. I sometimes think you don't care one way or another. I sometimes feel like you don't care about me."

"That's nonsense," he claimed nonchalantly.

"Is it?" I stared into Aram's eyes. He looked back at me, but with less conviction.

"It is nonsense."

"I wish I could believe that," I said as I turned away from him. "I really do." I cried a little while my back was to Aram but my anger overcame my sadness. I snapped back around to face him. "Let me ask you this…"

"What?" he interrupted, obviously annoyed.

"How did you feel before we came to the pet store today?"

"What do you mean?"

"I mean, how did you feel? Were you happy, sad…what?"

"I suppose I felt OK," he replied.

"Did you feel OK about us?"

"You're talking in circles," he said.

"Just answer the question."

"Did I feel OK about us? I suppose I did," he claimed.

"You don't sound too confident. Are you sure?" A long pause followed my question. I watched Aram as he shifted his weight from his right leg to his left, all the while he continued to look directly at me. I couldn't tell if he was annoyed, disinterested, or genuinely trying in some way to determine the answer to my question. "Well?" I asked after I tired of waiting.

"I'm sure, Kiley. I feel good about us."

"So somewhere underneath all your boorishness, you do care?"

"I said that I did."

"Are you sure you care about me? Are you sure you want a future with me?" I asked while peering into his eyes.

"Why would I be with you if I didn't?"

CHAPTER 28
WE CAN'T DO THIS

Ashley Morrison

"What are you doing here? Are you crazy?" I asked. Aram's eyes stared back into mine without concern as he smiled.

"I had to see you," he said.

"Goddamn it, Aram. Why are you doing this? You shouldn't have come here." I heard the panic in my own voice as I spoke.

"I'm tired of doing what I should do," he relayed calmly.

I opened the door wide enough for Aram to enter the house. "Well hurry up before someone sees you," I ordered. Aram moved past me slowly, taking a moment to glance at me as his shoulder brushed mine. I didn't know what to expect or what to say. I closed my eyes to gather myself as I shut the front door.

"Why are you here?" I asked in an emotionless voice.

"It's good to see you too, Ash."

"Cut the bullshit. What do you want?"

"Why are you being a bitch?" he asked. I could sense his carefree disposition shift as he tried to assess whether my temperament was genuine or obligatory. He couldn't possibly be sure which, because I wasn't.

"Aram, you can't just drop by my house. Do you forget that I'm engaged to William and *he lives here too?* Jesus…"

"I haven't forgotten your situation. I also haven't forgotten what happened between us the last time I was here. I haven't been able to stop thinking about it, actually."

"I thought you said you wouldn't do anything to hurt me?"

"I did, and I meant it," Aram claimed.

"Aram, you're hurting me right now. You're not respecting my situation or the person I love."

"I've always respected you."

"Don't start on these circular arguments. I'm engaged. You have a live-in girlfriend. This can't happen…" Aram interrupted me.

"It already has happened."

"That was a mistake." I didn't look away from him. I had to let him know I was serious.

"What happened between us was no mistake, Ash. You know it's true. This," he paused and gestured his hands to direct my attention to the house, "is a mistake."

"There you go… This is what I'm talking about. You think you know my situation. Shit, you think you know me, but you don't. Do you get it? You don't know me any longer, Aram. I've changed!" I felt like crying, but I didn't.

"What has changed about you?" he asked.

"I just want something different out of life. I need someone else"

"How can you say that? I mean really, how can you say such shit to my face after I was inside you just a week ago? What are you so afraid of? Are you afraid of feeling? Is that it?" he asked in a loud voice.

"I don't feel anything anymore," I said in a flat voice.

"You can feel, Ash. You felt for me before. It can happen again. We can forget about the last three years and live together happily." His eyes stared at me with such intensity I couldn't maintain eye contact any longer.

"I'm going to marry, William," I said in the same flat tone.

"You're afraid to be happy, aren't you? That's it!"

"I'm afraid to be hurt again. That's why I don't feel anything any longer. Do you get it now? I had to quit caring to regain any semblance of sanity and stability."

"It hasn't been easy for either of us, Ash. Quit being so self-centered."

"I love William, Aram. Listen to my words. I love him." I spoke in a slowed voice to emphasize the point.

"What about us? What about last time?" Aram persisted.

"What about last time? Last time I told you what happened represented a moment of personal weakness. It was closure. I hoped it would be closure for the both of us. It happened, it's over, and now I've moved on. I'm sorry."

"You're not sorry," Aram snapped back.

"I'm sorry that you're upset. I didn't want that to happen. I mean it. But there is no *us*. We're not starting over. How else can I say this so you'll understand? What happened wasn't anything but cheating."

"It didn't feel like cheating to me," Aram imparted.

"It should have, Aram. That's what it was. You cheated on your girlfriend. What would happen if she found out?" I looked at Aram intently.

"I don't care."

"Well, that's sad. It's sad you're OK with hurting other people."

"I don't need a moral lesson from you. Did you even wash the sheets before your love returned? Or did you sleep on the evidence? Is that benevolent concern to you?"

"Why are you doing this?"

"You're doing this," he retorted.

"You sleep next to your girlfriend every night and you have the audacity to persist with this shit... I can't believe it."

"No matter how you label it, this is still about us. This has always been about us. Even if you marry William, you'll still think of me. He doesn't make love to you like I used to, like I still do," Aram claimed confidently.

"What does that matter? That's such a guy comment. Sex doesn't make a relationship, at least not a mature one."

"It matters... It matters because he can't love you the way that I can."

"I don't need that kind of love anymore." Aram didn't say anything else. He only smiled at me from across the room. "What?" I asked. Aram didn't respond. He just stared and smiled.

"You're going to have to leave," I finally said. "William's going to be home soon."

"I'm not giving up on you. You know that, right?" I held the door open and Aram eventually began walking toward me.

"Goodbye, Aram." He stopped right in front of me. "I'm sorry," I said again.

"Goodbye, Ashley," he stated in a soft tone. Aram leaned down to kiss me and I turned away.

"Don't," I demanded. Aram didn't say anything. He leaned down again and I turned away again. "I said..." Aram grabbed my face and his lips met mine. I squirmed but he held me so tightly I couldn't break free. He pushed me against the wall. I felt his tongue enter my mouth. I kissed back. I had no idea why, other than it felt good and it turned me on. Just as I felt my face flush, Aram broke from me. He stood in front of me looking down at me as I struggled to regain my breath. Aram didn't say one word. He just stared intently into my eyes and then suddenly walked out.

CHAPTER 29
JAKOB'S PROMISE

Turner Brennan

I must have turned three shades of red when I turned around in the art store wearing a black top hat and a large fake mustache to see a dark, handsome boy staring at me. He smiled at me as I scrambled to tear the mustache off. I smiled back, temporarily forgetting I was still wearing the top hat. I reached for it and took it off as quickly as possible once I remembered. I slung it on the heap of costumes beside me as I watched him approaching.

"You know, I think I like the hat," he said to me as he smiled.

"You'll have to excuse me. I'm an idiot," I said, still embarrassed.

"It's cute." I couldn't look away from his blue eyes. "Do you go to school here?"

"I do... Well I do some days. Other days I don't. I suppose it all depends on the class and my mood."

"What a great answer. I go here too. I'm a junior."

"Sophomore here," I relayed.

"I don't mean to be forward... Well, actually I suppose I do. Either way, would you want to get together sometime?"

"I don't know. What's in it for me?" I asked in a serious tone.

"Excuse me?" he said, confused.

"Well, you see, I've picked out this large canvas that I want to purchase, but I can't carry it home. If you'd be willing to help me get it to my apartment, I would be willing to see you sometime. And I promise I will not be wearing a top hat."

"Or a mustache?"

"No facial hair either. What do you say?"

"How could I refuse? What's your name?"

"Turner. What's yours?" I asked.

"Jakob. It's nice to meet you, Turner."

"Likewise, Jakob. Did you drive here?"

I didn't feel as though I was really helping at all as Jakob struggled with the large canvas that proved awkward enough to deliver to my apartment without me getting in the way.

"Thank you so much for this," I said as he leaned the canvas against my living room wall.

"Is this where you want it?" he asked.

"That's fine. I'm not even sure what I'm going to do with it yet. I had to have it, though. You know?"

He laughed. "Yeah I do." I caught his blue eyes studying me. "Say, what are you doing Saturday?"

"I never think that far ahead," I answered.

"Ha-ha, well it is Thursday, so I thought you may have an idea."

"None whatsoever," I smiled after I spoke.

"Oh, OK."

"Why do you ask, Jakob?" I watched him closely, not allowing him to regain his composure at all.

"I…um…well, I was going to ask… You're not easy to approach," he said while laughing nervously.

"Nothing worthwhile is easy, Jakob."

"I suppose that's true. In that case, would you like to meet up again?" he asked finally.

"Sure… If I ever feel the need to purchase a large canvas, I will now know someone to help me drag it home," I joked.

"That's not exactly what I meant, but I guess that will work," Jakob said, unsure whether I was being facetious or not.

"I'm kidding," I finally revealed. "Of course we could meet up again. Anything is possible." Jakob laughed nervously. "What's your number?" I asked as I extracted my phone from my pocket. I never carried a purse.

"It's 291-5741," he quickly relayed.

"Wait a second… OK, what are the last four digits?"

"5-7-4-1," he restated, slower than before.

"OK, you're in my phone. Don't you feel special?"

"Of course I do." There was an awkward silence where I could sense Jakob struggling to think of something to say. "There's not a chance you're going to erase that number after I leave, is there?"

"Now, Jakob…what kind of person would I be if I did that? I mean, you did help me with this large canvas I may or may not use, right?"

"I sure did."

"Then I would be damn rude if I didn't at least call you at some point."

"I had to be sure."

"I understand. Women can be bitches," I said while watching him squirm under my watchful gaze.

"You said it, not me." I could tell he was nervous.

"It's OK to agree. It's true. Women can be bitches. It's a fact."

Jakob laughed again. His laughter ended and again silence resumed.

"Say…" he began, still trying to gain confidence. "It's taking every ounce of self-control I possess to keep from kissing you." He quit staring at the ground long enough to look up at me in order to gauge my response.

"Is that so?" I asked in an attempt to prolong his discomfort.

"It is," he confessed.

"I never indicated an aversion to the idea, I don't believe." Jakob's eyebrows raised. "I guess if you don't try, you'll never know," I eventually disclosed.

"Are you saying…?"

"Jakob, there are some moments in life that don't require words." As I finished speaking I kept my eyes on him as he walked slowly towards me. A rush of adrenaline coursed through me. I couldn't tell if the exhilaration had been initiated by the circumstance or by Jakob. I suppose the cause didn't matter.

CHAPTER 30
RYAN'S PLACE

Kiley Adams

Ryan answered the door shirtless, wearing nothing but jeans that hung low enough on his hips to clearly indicate he wasn't wearing underwear. He motioned me inside without saying a word. His hair looked disheveled. I couldn't tell if he styled it that way on purpose or not. Ryan usually wore boxer briefs unless he had just had sex or was planning on having it. *Which scenario had I stepped into?*

He walked toward me as I stood by the large window in his living room. He pulled me near, kissing my neck and then my cheek. I pushed both of my forearms against his chest in order to create some space between us. "Don't be that way, baby," he said in a low voice.

"Ryan, stop. I came here to talk to you," I pleaded.

"You came here for more than that," he said while kissing my neck and earlobe. I froze for a moment before I regained my strength.

"Seriously," I said in a louder tone.

"Jesus Christ, Kiley. What is it? Why the hell are you freaking out?"

"I'm not," I said. "I need to talk to you."

"I'm sick of talking. That's all we do any more is talk. What's in it for me? I don't need to talk about anything." He let go of me and walked away as he used his right hand to comb through his tousled hair.

"You smell different," I said after detecting an unfamiliar scent.

"Kiley, if you have something to say, would you goddamn just say it," Ryan groaned while turning to face me.

"Please don't be that way, Ryan."

"Just say whatever you need to say."

"We can't do this," I blurted.

"Do what?" he asked, annoyed.

"This! We can't keep meeting like this and pretending like we're not."

"It's nothing to get worked up about."

"I'm with Aram," I inserted.

"And?"

"That's the reason."

"Kiley, you're like a damn child sometimes. I know you're with Aram."

"I can't do this anymore."

"That's just it, Kiley. You are the one doing it. I don't visit you. Hell, I don't even know where you live. Frankly, I don't care. It is what it is."

"That's really kind of you, Ryan. You don't care about anyone but yourself, do you?"

"Why are you attacking me? You shouldn't be angry with me. I'm only giving you what you want."

"You're a dick."

"You like it."

"Shut up, Ryan. You don't care." I started to cry, even though I tried not to.

"Here we go with the tears."

"I'm with Aram," I said between sobs.

"I don't care if you are or aren't. Does Aram know I'm fucking you?"

"Don't," I implored.

"Well, does he? Does he know you like it?"

"Don't do this," I begged.

"Does he know you come over here and get what he can't give you? Does he not pull your hair like I do? Does he not leave your legs shaking?" His voice gained volume as he spoke.

"I can't take this."

"You can't take anything, Kiley. You're always a fucking mess and the saddest part is that the mess is your own creation." He paused for a moment and watched me cry. His eyes glared at me without an ounce of discernible care. "You disgust me."

"Then why…" I couldn't finish without sobbing. "Then why do you still see me? You have to feel something."

"I don't feel anything for you. That's why you keep coming back to me. It's good sex and nothing more. That's the truth. I don't know why you're crying; you've known that all along." I collapsed on the sofa and cried with my hands covering my face. Ryan didn't attempt to console me. He only stood over me and studied me curiously. It was as though he relished my misery.

"I'm glad I didn't have your child," I finally yelled.

"I never wanted you to have my child," he replied calmly.

"You're a monster. You're a monster because you don't care about anyone."

"I'm honest. I don't fake it like you do. If you care for Aram, would you really be over here with me crying on my sofa? Have you thought about that? Who's the real monster?"

"It's over, Ryan. I'm never going to see you again. You're a fucking waste." I took a deep breath and then yelled, "It's over! Do you hear me?"

"I hear you just fine, Kiley."

"I'm serious!"

"Are you?"

CHAPTER 31
SOMEDAY

Turner Brennan

Just as I was about to doze off for the second time that lonely Saturday afternoon in late May, I heard someone at the door. I stood up and glanced at my appearance in the mirror. I patted my head in an attempt to flatten the hideous waves in my hair caused by the pillow. I stepped away from the mirror and then stepped back to make sure before I scrambled to open my door. I felt the breath escape from me. Aram stood before me in dark jeans and a blue, pearl-snap, long-sleeve shirt that made him look thin and fit. I wanted to hug him right away, but I refrained from doing so.

"How do you do, Turner?" he asked in a low, sexy voice.

"I do quite well, Aram," I replied in a tone that was intended to sound playful, but instead sounded dorky. I stood, paralyzed, thinking of how Aram probably thought I was stupid.

"Can I come in?" he asked while staring at me.

"Oh, yes… Please… You'll have to excuse my manners. I don't get visitors often." Aram chuckled as he walked past. I looked down at his ass as he walked by. It looked so tight in his jeans that I had to consciously keep my hands from reaching out to squeeze it. "So what do I owe the pleasure?"

"I was in the neighborhood," he responded.

"I suppose I should consider myself a lucky girl then."

"Lucky indeed." He walked past my kitchen and stood in my living room. He appeared to have forgotten how small my apartment really was. I felt panicked when I noticed that my box of recently purchased tampons were in plain sight underneath my desk. Luckily, he didn't appear to notice. "So what are you up to today?" he asked.

"Oh, you know, just preparing for another eventful Saturday evening."

"Is that so?" he glanced around the room. "What do you have planned?"

"Well, before you came over I was preparing to revisit naptown. One nap just didn't feel sufficient today. You know?"

"Ha-ha. I do know. We all have those days."

"Do you have any plans today?" I hated that I sounded so desperate.

"Not really. I haven't seen you or talked to you. I was beginning to think you had forgotten me."

I wanted to kneel down before him and grab his hand before solemnly swearing to him that could never happen. Instead I looked away. "So can I assume you had forgotten me then?"

"Don't say crazy things, Aram. That's not even possible."

"Whew," he wiped his hand over his brow jokingly. "I had hoped that wasn't the case."

Aram sat on my bed and looked out the window as I walked to the kitchen to pour him a glass of water. "Can I ask you something?" I yelled from the kitchen, feeling a bit more secure since I couldn't see his reaction.

"Sure," he yelled back. I walked from the kitchen with two glasses of water in my hands. I gave one to Aram and then sat next to him on the bed.

"Don't you love this street? It's always so busy. I adore it."

"I do love it. Was that what you wanted to ask?"

"No… I don't know how to say it."

"What, Turner?"

"Can I just say it?" I wasn't at all sure what overcame me, but I felt I had to tell Aram the truth.

"Feel free. You can always tell me what you're thinking."

"Okay…" I paused as I gathered my thoughts but they only remained scattered remnants of coherence. "I don't know how to say this so I'm just going to say it," I said, partly to delay the confession further. "I like you," I finally blurted. I didn't want to look at Aram, but I had to as I awaited his response.

"I like you too," he said without hesitation.

"You do?"

"Of course I do, Turner. I wouldn't be here with you right now if I didn't." I smiled. I sat next to Aram in silence. I wanted him to expound on the topic but he didn't.

"I really like you, Aram. I mean, I don't know what to do."

"What do you mean?"

"I know you're with Kiley. I'm not trying to say anything about your relationship." I couldn't help but cringe as I said the words. If only Aram knew how much I hated her. "I can't deny how I feel any longer. I think about you all the time."

"I'm honored, Turner." There was a pause that felt like days. "I don't know what else to say."

"Do you think about me?" I couldn't help but ask.

"Of course I do," he said.

"What do we do?" I asked.

"What do you mean?"

"Could you ever be with me? I mean, I know I'm young…"

"Turner, we can't," he interrupted.

"Why not?"

"Because," he said before pausing. "I'm with Kiley."

"Do you love her?" I asked, feeling like it may be my only opportunity to pose the question I desperately wanted him to answer.

"I don't really know."

"Then you don't," I said confidently. "If you loved her, you'd know. There would be no uncertainty at all."

"Maybe you're right," he said in a solemn tone.

"I know I'm right. There may be quite a bit I don't know, but I know I'm right about this." I sat the glass of water on the floor and leaned back in bed, feeling both relief and frustration.

"So what now?" I finally asked.

"I don't know," he said.

"Why can't we be together? Is it only because of Kiley?" I asked Aram. He paused.

"Yes," he finally answered.

"So otherwise we could potentially be together?"

"Maybe, someday. Who knows?" I leaned forward and kissed his cheek as soon as I heard the words. "What was that for?" he asked.

"That was for the opportunity. That's all I could ever ask of you."

"You're amazing," he said.

"You know I'd do anything for you, right?" I said in a serious tone.

"I do know that, Turner. You're the greatest. That's why you're my girl."

"Oh yeah?"

"Yeah. You're absolutely wonderful in every way."

I kissed his mouth until I felt his lips gripping mine with the same enthusiasm. His right hand cupped the back of my head as his tongue entered my mouth. He held me still as his tongue flicked against mine. I cherished the closeness as I felt his grip tighten. He tugged my hair gently, pulling my head back enough that my neck became exposed. He broke from my lips and kissed my neck, first with his lips and then the tip of his tongue touched my skin ever so softly. I opened my eyes and looked at him as he approached me again. This time both of my hands pulled his face near and we kissed deeply. I couldn't get enough of his touch, his taste, his scent. I imagined how alive I would forever feel if he were mine. I thought about the love letters I'd leave on his pillow after I left the apartment. I thought about the dinners we would share talking about art and music. I thought about dancing with Aram in a lonely street where the only audience would be the passersby who would look at us as if we were the last romantics left. Aram reached for me and brought me closer. I undid his pants and then broke from our kissing. He needed me. That was enough for now.

CHAPTER 32
CONFUSED

Ashley Morrison

I saw Aram before he noticed me in the diner on Omaha and Eighteenth Street. I watched him carefully part his way through the people standing in line at the register waiting to pay for their meals. I admired the ease of his walk as he excused himself politely. A few women stared at him as he sauntered by. It didn't bother me. I found myself doing the exact same thing. There was something unique about him. Some might call it a mystique; others might call it a raw sexuality. Either way, I had never met anyone like him before and I seriously doubted I would meet anyone like him again. When he saw me his eyes became alive and the rest of the diner no longer appeared to matter to him. I couldn't help smiling. Aram Young would forever be my first true love.

He slid casually into the booth across from me and smiled. I smiled back at him. In fact, I don't think I had stopped smiling since the first moment I noticed him enter the diner. His hands rested comfortably on the table. I felt my mouth get dry. I couldn't stop looking at him.

"Thank you for coming," I said. "I realize the last time I saw you I was a complete bitch."

"You knew I'd be here. Did you even question it?"

"No I didn't and I can't tell you how much that means. I don't know... I've been a mess lately," I admitted.

"It's OK, Ash. I understand everything has been a bit stressful, to say the least. I'm just glad I am here with you now."

"I'm glad too," I admitted. Aram reached across the table and squeezed my hand. I should have pulled away from his grip but I didn't.

"So how are you?" he asked as he withdrew his hand from mine.

"I've been better. I don't know. I don't really want to get into it."

"Why did you want to meet me?" he asked, appearing to be a bit confused.

"I don't know. I guess to apologize. I guess I just needed to see you to know that you're OK."

"Of course I'm OK. I forgave you as soon as it happened. I truly did."

"I don't know how to thank you."

"You don't have to. Isn't it nice to not feel any obligations? All you have to do is be yourself around me. That's all I could ever ask." I couldn't stop smiling.

We ordered two coffees and drank them slowly as we enjoyed each other's company. We didn't talk too much. Every once in a while Aram's eyes would meet mine and we would both grin like innocent children. Somehow I had forgotten how those moments have the propensity to make everything matter again.

"I want a cigarette. Would you want to go outside with me?"

"Sure. Are you done with your coffee?"

"Yeah." Aram leaned forward and dug into his pocket. He extracted six dollars and placed them on the table under his mug.

"Let's go," he said as he stood up. I followed him out the door, feeling his hand press against the small of my back.

* * *

Emotions always confused me. I could never decipher what they ever meant, if anything. All I knew was that when Aram came over after our visit at the diner, I felt like life mattered again. We didn't talk. As soon as I closed the front door the kissing started and before either of us consciously considered the potential for disaster to ensue, he had me against the wall and was pulling at my clothes. We moved to the bedroom where we both disrobed quickly. Our frantic attempt to reveal ourselves entirely to the other only heightened the excitement. We kissed deeply. Aram sucked my lower lip. I gently bit his upper lip and that's when he pulled my head back by my hair and kissed my neck. I felt my breath escape from me as he continued working his way down my neck to my breasts. At that moment, I stopped thinking.

I rested beside Aram in bed and heaved heavy breaths after it was over. I looked over at him and found him staring at the ceiling, a big grin on his face.

"What are you thinking about?" I asked.

"You," he said in a low voice.

"What about me?"

"You'll never know," he relayed. I wasn't sure what he meant. It didn't matter. I moved closer so that I could feel Aram's body next to mine. His skin felt warm to the touch and was still moist from perspiration. I would have to remember to wash the sheets after he left. I traced Aram's abdomen with my forefinger like I used to do years ago after we made love. I loved the way his body responded to my touch as his muscles tightened.

Aram rose from bed when his phone started ringing. He picked up his jeans from the floor and dug in the front pocket until he retrieved it. I heard Aram say, "Shit," once he saw who was calling. I started to panic a bit and decided to pull the sheets off the bed and stick them in the washer. When I returned, I found Aram sitting on my mattress shaking his head as he listened. "OK, I heard you the first time," Aram said. "I'll be there soon enough. Don't get so upset." He ended the call and immediately started getting dressed.

"Was that her?" I asked. I don't know why I felt compelled to do so.

"Who?" he asked, noticeably distracted.

"Kiley?"

"Oh, yeah. She says we have to talk." I felt bad, as if somehow she knew about us.

"I'm sorry," I expressed.

Aram walked toward me. He kissed my forehead. "Don't be," he said. He touched my chin so that I would look up at him. I did. "I don't ever regret being with you." His statement should have made me feel better, but it didn't.

"I don't want you to get in any trouble over this. I shouldn't have asked you to meet me. I'm not sure what my problem is. I keep fucking everything up."

"Ash, stop! Don't say that."

"It's not right, Aram," I said while looking at him. "We can't pretend that it is."

"Who's to say it isn't?"

"It just isn't. Do you think she knows?" I felt a sickening feeling overcome me.

"I don't care if she does."

CHAPTER 33
JAKOB'S APARTMENT

Turner Brennan

"I didn't know you paint." I studied the canvases strewn about Jakob's apartment. Some were completed pieces, while others remained unfinished. His talent made me feel somewhat ashamed he had seen my work.

"You never asked," he stated. "There's really nothing to mention."

"Are you kidding me?" I interjected. "These are beautiful." I walked from one painting to the next, studying each one. The brush strokes were refined, yet full of energy.

"You're too nice," he coyly commented.

"Nonsense! You're talented." His embarrassment became apparent by the way he avoided looking at me or commenting any further.

I had looked at a number of his canvases while he busied himself with his music collection. He said he was trying to select an album he thought I would enjoy. His preoccupation with pleasing me felt foreign, though I must admit, I found it adorable. He finally settled on a musician I had never heard of before.

"Close your eyes," he said. "These songs make more sense that way." I did as he asked and closed my eyes right where I stood. "Can you envision it?"

"I can," I said with my eyelids still firmly closed. "It's uncanny."

"I know. I'm not sure how or why it works, but it does. Maybe it has something to do with the rhythm created by the syllables. I'm not sure."

"Yeah, I have no clue." I stayed in that position until the song finished. Afterward I felt calmer and I noticed that Jakob appeared to be more tranquil as well.

He promised me that he would cook dinner, but as I studied his kitchen, it became quite apparent that he rarely cooked.

"Where are all your pans and cooking utensils?" I asked in an attempt to refute his claims that he was an accomplished chef.

"I don't need fancy utensils to create a masterful dish," he said while smiling.

"I'm more worried about the dish being functionally edible."

"Ye of little faith. I suppose I'll have to prove you wrong."

"Please do, good sir," I joked.

As he worked to thaw the meat for spaghetti by submerging the package of ground turkey in the sink he had filled with scalding water, I filled his only pot with water and placed it on the stove.

"Use a spoon, silly," I said in response to watching Jakob poke at the package with his finger in an effort to submerge it briefly in the hot water before he found himself forced to repeat the task.

"Aren't you a smart helper?"

"Helper? If I left you to accomplish this task alone, you'd surely maim yourself." Jakob laughed.

"Touché, smart girl."

"Don't forget beautiful."

"And crazy," he added.

Despite the fact that I did the majority of the work, I allowed Jakob to take credit for the meal. He procured two old, battered ceramic plates from the kitchen cabinet and looked them over before handing me one. I looked it over again, partly to check for cleanliness, and partly to study the intricate design painted on them. Jakob used two spoons to pile the pasta on our plates. He claimed that he possessed tongs, but we couldn't find them. He then spread the marinara sauce over the noodles on my plate before doing the same on his plate. I watched with horror at the amount he gave me.

"I can't eat all of this," I claimed. "I'm not a boy."

"Just eat what you can. We can save the rest."

I waited on Jakob to finish preparing his plate because I didn't know where he wanted to sit. I followed him to the living room where I stood as he fiddled with the music once more.

"Do you want to sit in here?" he asked.

"Sure, why not?" I responded.

"What would you like to drink?" He sat his plate down next to the stereo as he prepared to revisit the kitchen.

"Water would be fine," I said.

"Coming right up." He walked into the kitchen as I sat down in his cushy recliner. I feared making a mess and became even more panicked when I realized my button-down shirt was light blue. I was notorious for leaving stains on such vulnerably colored tops. What made the idea so frightful in that setting was that someone else, whose opinion I surmised at last somehow mattered to me, could potentially become aware of this personal flaw. I decided, as I heard him returning to the living room, that I would eat as slowly and as carefully as humanly possible, even if it meant that I remained hungry after the meal.

Luckily I escaped dinner stain free.

"You have a little something…" Jakob said as he motioned toward my face.

"Oh, how embarrassing," I said jokingly as I wiped around the mess.

"You're the most beautiful clown I could ever imagine," Jakob claimed.

"No nicer words have ever been said."

I took my plate into the kitchen and turned around only to bump into Jakob. He instinctively brought me into him as a means to maintain balance.

"I'm sorry," I said before I noticed I hadn't moved away from him.

"It's quite OK." He held me next to him and I remained unable to move away. Inexplicably he leaned toward me at the same time that I leaned into him and our lips met. We kissed slowly. His lips gripped mine as he held me. Jakob wanted me. I could tell by the tender way he kissed me in the kitchen. I wanted him too, if for no other reason than it felt good to be wanted by another person. I wasn't sure if it was right, but I wasn't sure if it was wrong either.

"Can I have this dance?" Jakob asked as we sat on the floor in his living room listening to music.

"Excuse me?"

"I'm formally requesting a dance, if you'll indulge me, of course."

"Well, it would be damn rude of me to resist," I said, finding myself enjoying our banter. I stood and took Jakob's outstretched hand in my own. One hand gripped mine gently and his other arm drew me closer to him. He moved back and forth as his arm tightened around my waist. I closed my eyes and let him lead my body in a slow circle. I loved how lost I felt in that moment.

Before either one of us was aware of it, we found that it was well past one in the morning. Our talks about which paint brushes work the best, techniques for cleaning the bristles, the moronic state of pop music, and an overall apprehension associated with ever fully growing up caused the time to pass unusually fast.

"I better go," I finally said while standing up from my position on the carpet.

"You don't have to," Jakob said, followed by a nervous smile.

"That's awfully kind of you, but I better," I reaffirmed.

"It's up to you," he said, sounding a bit disheartened. "I wish that you would stay though."

"I'm actually surprised you're not throwing me out already," I said, half-jokingly.

"How could I kick a girl out who still has red tomato sauce around her lips?" I instinctively placed my hand over my mouth to shield it from sight. "Just kidding," he said while giggling.

"Not funny," I said in a muffled voice with my hand still securely over my mouth. I walked through the hallway until I came to his bathroom. I turned the light on and removed my hand to find that he had indeed been kidding. "You jerk," I yelled from the bathroom. "That's mean."

"You have to admit it was funny." Jakob had followed me and stood in the doorway of the bathroom.

"Maybe for you, but not for me," I said, acting as though I was truly upset.

"Don't take everything so seriously," Jakob said as he tried to ascertain if I was really upset, or merely acting.

"I suppose you're right," I said as I made faces at him in the mirror. He returned a few faces at me that caused me to laugh. "I don't retract my statement though. You really are a jerk." I observed Jakob's reflection moving closer to mine.

"Is that so?"

"It is. You're a big, fat jerk." I felt his lips on my cheek. "I mean it. Don't try to persuade me otherwise."

"I would…" His lips kissed my cheek again. "Never do…" He kissed my ear. "That… ever." I turned to face Jakob. His lips met mine and we kissed tenderly. Jakob pulled my body close to his. "Are you sure you can't stay?" he asked.

"You're making it hard to decline the offer," I said between kisses.

"That's my intention," he whispered.

"Do you think we should?" I asked him, feeling my body aching for more.

"Why not?"

CHAPTER 34
WHAT'S WRONG?

Kiley Adams

I knew something was wrong when Aram returned home from work. It wasn't anything he said. It was the way he avoided me that caused me to draw that conclusion. He didn't look at me as he opened the front door and when I said hello he only looked at me as he walked by to the bedroom. His distance would come and go at times, but what frightened me so much about his demeanor was the overwhelming sense of indifference he displayed. Everything about him suggested that nothing mattered.

"What did you want when you called?" he yelled from the bedroom. I could hear him changing and hanging his dress clothes in the closet.

"I'll tell you when you finish," I relayed, trying to summon the courage to do so. I waited impatiently as he fumbled in the bedroom. I heard him enter the bathroom. He turned the water on and I heard him washing his hands before he turned the water off. When he entered the room, he was still drying his hands. *Why did he wash his hands?*

"So what did you need earlier?" he asked while looking in my direction. He couldn't look directly at me for some reason.

"I wouldn't have bothered you unless it was important. You know that, right?" I asked, unsure of how to preface what I was about to tell him.

"What is it, Kiley? Let's not play any games."

"You may want to sit down," I said, stalling.

"I'm fine," he said coldly. "What is it?"

"I don't know how to tell you," I admitted.

"Well, I have something to tell you too," he said. My heart stopped for a moment.

"What?" I asked as my mind raced.

"Kiley, I don't think this is working. I mean, we both know our relationship has kind of been deteriorating lately."

"I can't believe what I'm hearing," I said in a hushed voice.

"Why can't you believe it?" he asked. "Because you don't want to? Kiley, let's not lie to each other. More importantly, let's not lie to ourselves. We aren't working as a couple. It's as simple as that. It's just not working."

"I can't believe this," I repeated, unable to say anything else.

"Why do you keep saying that?"

"Because we are working," I expressed. "I don't think our relationship has been deteriorating. What would make you say such a thing?"

"It's true. Why are you refusing to accept the truth?"

"It's not true," I retorted.

"Kiley..."

"Stop it, Aram. You're going through some damn crisis, that's all. It's not us, it's *you*!"

"I don't think so."

"You haven't had any trouble making love to me or sleeping next to me at night."

"That doesn't make a relationship, Kiley," he replied.

"Oh, it doesn't? You can separate sex from love and companionship? Are you even fucking human? Why have you shut down lately?

Are you fucking someone else?" My voice elevated until I found myself screaming.

"Calm down, Kiley."

"Calm down? You want me to calm down? You're standing before me claiming that our relationship is over, telling me casually that our lovemaking is mechanical and meaningless, and I'm supposed to calm down? You're such an arrogant prick. You really don't care about anyone but yourself, do you? I should have known you'd react this way. I always feared you never knew what love is."

"Do you know what love is?" he asked.

"I know you lack the capacity. You're too damn self-involved to ever love anyone but yourself. I feel sorry for you. You're cursed to endure a lonely existence unless you change."

"Is that so?"

"You don't even care do you? That's the most frightening aspect. You've completely given up on love. You've given up on being human."

"If you say so."

"Is that all you have to say? Everything we've been building for the last year is crumbling and that's all you have to say? God, you're so damn miserable you have to make everyone around you miserable, don't you?"

"I don't know what to say, Kiley. You don't see it."

"See what?"

"The fucking problems with us."

"The problems are with *you!*"

"Whatever. I'm going to go ahead and leave if we're finished here."

"Fuck you, Aram," I said as I started to cry. "I hope you're happy now."

"With what?"

"I'm as miserable as you are. See…we do have something in common: misery."

"Oh, quit being melodramatic, Kiley."

"Just fucking leave. That's what you want to do, so do it. Quit being a pussy and do it."

"Goodbye, Kiley." He waved his hand halfheartedly as he turned to walk out of the living room and out of my life. I couldn't contain my sadness any longer. I stood up to stop him and almost collapsed.

"Wait!" I yelled.

"What," he said as he turned around to face me. He saw my face and was forced to confront my reddened eyes as the tears steadily rolled down my cheeks. "Kiley, don't be this way."

"I can't help it, Aram. I'm sad and when people are sad they cry. You would understand if you actually felt emotions."

"Maybe I've been hurt too much. I think I quit wanting to feel a long time ago."

"I feel sorry for you then. Feeling is what makes life livable. Emotions provide meaning," I said between sobs. All I wanted to do is reach out to Aram and pull him close.

"I never claimed that any of this had meaning. I don't know if anything has meaning anymore."

"Doesn't that make you sad?" I asked.

"I don't know. I guess it's just life."

"Aram, you can't leave this way."

"Kiley, I have to. I'm sorry." He turned away from me and opened the door.

"Aram, I'm pregnant," I finally said. He suddenly stopped where he stood.

"Excuse me?"

"I'm pregnant. That's what I wanted to tell you. That's why I've been so concerned about us lately. I'm going to have your child. Now do you feel something?"

"How long have you known?" he asked.

"Not very long," I said. He didn't say anything. "Will you stay? I need you."

"You don't need me, Kiley. No one really needs anybody else. It's just something people say. It's not true."

"Aram…" He turned away from me again and walked out the door.

CHAPTER 35
WILLIAM'S BIRTHDAY

Ashley Morrison

I thought I had been drinking for the past three years because I felt too much, because I missed Aram too much. It wasn't until that exact moment while sitting next to William that I realized Aram wasn't the reason at all. I had been drinking for the past three years, not because I felt too much, but because I felt nothing any longer.

"Thank you, sweetie," William said in a soft voice.

"For what?" I asked, temporarily confused.

"For organizing this party, for inviting all of my friends, for being you," he imparted sincerely. "You even invited Charles and you hate Charles."

"I hate all of your friends, honey," I said, half-kidding. William smiled.

"I love you. I really do. I can't wait until you're my wife." I looked at William as he smiled and took another drink from my glass of wine.

The dancing ensued and I got drunker as William and his friends made fools of themselves. I hadn't danced with him since the very beginning when a slow song played and he politely asked me in front of

151

his parents to join him. I obliged. After the song finished I sat down and only moved to flag a waitress whenever my glass need refilled with chardonnay.

"Baby, don't you want to dance with your old man?" William called to me from the dance floor.

"I'll sit this one out," I called back.

"Your loss." The top button on his shirt was undone and his tie hung loosely around his neck. Any other time I would have found him adorable. For whatever reason, at that moment, I couldn't make myself care. I stared at all of the people laughing and mingling. *Could everyone really be as happy as they appear? Or was it all a farce?* Nothing felt real any longer. It hadn't for quite some time. In less than two months, I'd be married and all I could consider at that moment was my own misery. *Why was I miserable?* I had everything I ever wanted.

I kept smiling, hoping that other people would refrain from speaking to me. I couldn't bear to feign interest in conversation with anyone at William's birthday party. Everyone was a stranger. Sure, the faces appeared familiar, but I didn't really know any of them and none of them really knew me. My hell had become an alienation that felt all too comfortable.

"Ashley…Ash, come over here," William yelled to me. "John wants a picture of all of us." I arose from my seat, feeling the lightheadedness hit me immediately as I clung to the table to maintain my balance. All I could hope for was that I wouldn't fall down on the walk over to William. My mouth felt numb from the wine. I brushed my hair from my face and slowly walked over. When I finally made it to the group, no one even noticed my drunkenness. Everyone was drunk. I fit right in.

As I stood next to William waiting for Charles to snap the photo, I thought for a second I was going to get sick. I tugged on William's arm.

"I want to leave soon," I told William.

"What?" he asked over the commotion.

"Never mind," I said, feeling the nausea waning. William's attention was quickly diverted from me.

"Everyone make a stupid face!" Charles shouted above the music and the swirling dialogues. William put his arm around me and squeezed me tightly as the camera flashed. I wondered who would see the picture. *How would I appear?*

"One more," Charles relayed. William let go of me. I remained close to him. A second flash and it was over. Everyone started milling around. William looked at me.

"Are you having fun?" he asked.

"Sure."

"Okay. I can't tell sometimes with you."

"Don't worry about me. I'm fine."

I quickly resumed my seat at the table while William bounded off to join his friends for more drinks and idiotic dancing to old pop songs. I asked the waitress to bring me another glass of chilled chardonnay. I figured if I drank the warm one on the table I might vomit it right back up.

"Aren't our men adorable?" Allison asked.

"Excuse me?" I heard her, but for some reason wanted to hear her ask the question again. I thought maybe the second time it would resonate differently. It didn't.

"Our men, they're adorable," she restated while staring at Tim, her husband.

"Yeah," I replied halfheartedly.

"So how's the wedding planning going?" I hated it when people asked about the planning.

"Good, I suppose."

"You have to be so excited. I remember how stressed out I was for my wedding but it was all worth it. It will be the best day of your life," she said while smiling to herself.

"Yeah. It's pretty stressful." All I could think about was that I hoped it wasn't the best day of my life. The idea sounded so pathetic.

"Just remember not to let the stress ruin the day. It's important to let go that day and simply enjoy it. It sounds impossible to do, but you have to. Everything will take care of itself by that time." I stared ahead, zoning out as Allison spoke.

I quit listening to Allison entirely. I just nodded my head and if she paused, I would say, "yeah," and wait for her to resume talking. *Would I ever paint again?* I used to paint all the time when I was with Aram. Ever since our breakup I had been caught up in trying to impress my mother and prove I had somehow grown up. I missed drinking wine and painting. Aram used to sit and watch me for hours as music played in the background. Those were the days I wished could last forever.

Allison soon excused herself and I found myself alone. I hated being alone. I could never get used to it. *Could I love William forever? How realistic was that notion? Did I still love Aram?* I guessed there would be no way of ever knowing. Love really is a daily decision.

CHAPTER 36
FLOWERS

Turner Brennan

A knock on the door caused me to stop painting. As I approached the door, I stopped for a second and turned back around in order to look at the canvas from a distance. A second knock came.

"Wait a second," I groaned. I opened the door to find a clean-cut guy in a uniform holding a bouquet of flowers.

"Miss Brennan?" he asked.

"Yes," I replied while staring at the flowers in his hand, each one in full bloom.

"These are for you," he said. "I need you to sign here." He held out a piece of paper attached to a clipboard. I took it from him and signed with the pen he provided. "You're all set," he said. "Have a great day."

"Thanks." I closed the door and lowered my face toward the outstretched blooms. The aroma was better than I imagined it would be. I closed my eyes to savor it. Then it struck me. I didn't know who had sent the lovely bouquet. As I walked to the kitchen to find a glass to put them in, I discarded the plastic wrapping around the stems in an attempt to find out who they were from. Surely there was a card or a sticker. I searched, but found nothing. *Who would've sent them to little old me?* It must have been Aram. The very thought made me feel warm and caused my stomach to turn from excitement.

I arranged the flowers in a blue glass I picked up at a garage sale years ago when I still lived with my parents. I loved how the blue hue interacted with the green stems. It made the stems appear almost as vibrant as the blooms. I placed them in my windowsill and admired them from a few feet, tilting my head slightly to gain the proper perspective. As I did so, another knock on my door sounded.

"Just a minute," I yelled as I again walked over to answer it.

"Surprise!" Jakob shouted as I opened the door. "How are you?" he asked as he looked at me smiling.

"What are you doing here?" I said, consciously noticing that I too was smiling.

"Swooping you up for an adventure. Are you game?"

"What adventure?" I asked, almost forgetting entirely about the flowers.

"I can't tell you until you agree to it."

"That's fair enough," I said looking at Jakob still standing in the doorway. "I'm in."

"Great! Grab your shit and let's go." I took one look around and remembered the flowers.

"I'm ready," I said emphatically in an attempt to usher Jakob away from my apartment so that he wouldn't see the flowers that Aram had sent. Jakob grabbed my hand and we hurriedly walked down the stairs and out of the building. Once outside the building it dawned on me that maybe Jakob sent the flowers and not Aram.

"Where are we going?" I asked, still gripping Jakob's hand as we crossed the street.

"I told you, it's a surprise."

"No, you told me you would tell me if I agreed to the adventure."

"OK, you're right. I want you to see this small antique store off Delaney Street."

"Why?" I asked.

"You'll see once we get there." Jakob pulled my hand as we dodged the oncoming traffic and barely made it to the other side of the street as passing cars blared their horns.

"Jakob! You're going to get us killed."

"Nonsense. We have the right-of-way."

"Not if we're breaking the law, you lunatic!"

"Oops…"

I had never been to the antique store off Delaney, primarily because Delaney Street scared me. There were always people in the street mumbling to themselves or others, and mostly in nonsensical ramblings that made me think they were in some way disturbed. I had avoided that part of town ever since I gave fifty cents to an older man seated against the building sleeping only to have him throw the quarters at me as I walked away. When I heard the quarters zipping past me and eventually clanking along the sidewalk, I turned to see the old man shaking a raised, balled fist in my direction and shouting profanities. That was all it took for me to avoid the area.

"Are you sure we should be here?" I asked, reliving the memory as we walked.

"Don't tell me you're one of those bourgeois stiffs that are afraid of diversity."

"How dare you," I said, realizing the apparent shock of my response was precipitated by my subconscious acknowledgement that he was right.

The antique store smelled like old dog and the carpet had a scratchy texture that caused a noise to emanate with every step. It caused my natural hesitation to become amplified. I followed Jakob as the floor creaked underfoot.

"Where is this surprise?" I asked in a low voice.

"Upstairs," he replied.

I eyed each step before I actually set foot on them in an attempt to determine if they would support my weight. I had horrible visions of myself slipping and tumbling down the whole staircase. I could feel the embarrassment welling within, even though it hadn't happened.

Surprisingly I made it without falling. As soon as I stepped into the tiny upstairs room my gaze zeroed in on it. Resting against the far wall was the perfect violet glass vase. I rushed over to it and knelt down to gently pick it up. I held it up so that I could look through the glass at the lights on the ceiling. The slivers of refracted light produced the most beautiful blend of colors.

"How did you know?" I said while still holding it up to the light.

"I had a good idea," he said.

"Well you were right. I love it!"

"I thought you would."

The exhilaration I felt while Jakob purchased the vase was quickly replaced by anxiety as I attempted to surmise his motive. *Why did he take me to the antique store specifically to purchase a vase? Did he do so because he sent me the flowers?* I tried to study his behaviors, looking for any small indicator that would provide a sufficient answer to my questions. He offered no insight.

"Thank you," I finally said. I eyed his response closely.

"For what?" he asked.

"You know." I waited, but he didn't respond in a telling manner. "The vase," I finally said to quell the uncomfortable silence between us. He smiled and gripped my hand tightly in his.

"You're welcome. I'm glad you like it."

We crossed the streets with less urgency but with more deliberate attention to each other. I could sense him looking at me from time to time. I liked the attention. Just as we approached my apartment, my phone sounded with a text. It was from Aram and simply said, "Where are you?" Maybe he sent the flowers after all.

CHAPTER 37
PARKING LOT

Ashley Morrison

When I finally arrived to meet Aram, it was five past ten in the evening. I was late. Aram should have considered himself lucky that I showed at all. I had to make up some bullshit excuse about needing to check prices on items for work, and luckily William didn't ask for any further details. I noticed Aram standing beside his car as I pulled into the lot and eased my car into the spot right next to him. The double life I was leading had begun to take its toll. I couldn't remember who I said what to, and frankly found myself not caring. I wanted to disappear forever. *Why couldn't I?*

Aram hugged me as soon as I got out of my car. I hugged him back, though my intensity didn't quite match his.

"So what did you need to talk to me about?" I asked, not sure why I had gone through all the effort to meet him.

"We need to talk," he said simply.

"About what?" I asked.

"Us."

"What about us?" I felt myself growing anxious at the prospect.

"What is happening between us?"

"What do you mean, Aram?"

"You know what I mean. Are you feeling what I'm feeling?"

"I don't know. What are you feeling?" I wanted to get sick.

"I'm in love with you, Ash. I never stopped loving you."

"Aram…"

"Wait…" he said, interrupting me. "Don't dismiss me like you typically do. You have to feel something. God, I've lumbered along for years now and for the first time I feel passionate about a cause again. I feel like we could make it if you'd just give us a chance."

"What are you not getting, Aram?" I asked, feeling my frustration mounting. "There is no us. I don't know what we've been doing…" He interrupted me again.

"We've been having an affair."

"I wouldn't call it that," I said.

"What would you call it, Ashley? We're fucking each other, aren't we? I haven't told Kiley. Have you told William?"

"Don't," I demanded.

"I don't know why you can't confront the issue and admit it."

"Admit what?"

"You don't love William."

"That's not true."

"Yes it is."

"You know what? You're so goddamn quick to judge everyone else. What about you, you fucking liar. Do you love Kiley?" Just saying her name made me cringe. I wasn't sure why.

"That's just it, Ash. I don't love her. I've been telling you that."

"Then why are you with her?"

"It's just what I'm doing… I guess it's my way to cope."

"Cope with what? Is that guy-talk meaning that you want someone to fuck?"

"No… I don't know… Maybe."

"Guys are disgusting," I said as I turned away from him.

"You're no better. The only difference between us is that I admit it while you lie to everyone, including yourself. You're not better. Our behavior is the same. Can't you see that? We're both cheaters."

"Stop it, Aram. You really know how to make me feel like shit."

"Am I the one making you feel like shit?"

"Who else would it be? Who else would even have that capacity?"

"You were always scared. That's why we broke up in the first place. You were always so fucking scared."

"Scared? Scared of what, you asshole?"

"You're scared of happiness. You're scared that if you really try to be happy that you might be disappointed so you spend your life living in misery because at least you can control being miserable. It's not a surprise to you. You know there might be something more, and that scares the shit out of you because that would mean that your misery is your own doing, not anyone else's. You would have to assume complete responsibility, and that horrifies you."

"You're always right, Aram. I don't even know why I talk to you. You never actually converse with anyone. You just talk at them. It's so fucking frustrating." I wanted to cry, but somehow I maintained my composure.

"Don't give me that victim mentality, Ashley. You love being the victim. You thrive on it. It's the passivity that allows you to assume no control or responsibility over your life. Goddamn, wake up, would you? We can be happy together."

"No we can't," I stated bluntly.

"You would never know. You quit. You always quit. Whenever something becomes too difficult or distressing, you just quit. That's what you do."

"You're right, Aram. You're always right. Well, I'm glad I drove all the way here to listen to this rant you've prepared. I hope you feel better. Now if you don't mind, I'm going to drive home and try to forget all about this."

"Wait!" he shouted at me. I instinctively looked around the vacant lot to see if anyone was around. We were still alone.

"Are you really going to leave like this?" Aram asked.

"Yes, Aram. It's what I do, remember?"

"Stop," he said as he gripped my arms firmly. "Ashley, will you look at me?" he pleaded in a softer voice.

"What?" I said as I turned around.

"Look at me. I want you to tell me to my face that you don't care about me." His eyes stared directly into mine. I felt a lump in my throat.

"Aram, you know I care about you."

"Do you love me?" he persisted.

"Why are you doing this?"

"Just answer me."

"I can't. You know I'm with William."

"Stop hiding behind excuses. Just answer me. Do you love me?"

"I…" a tear finally rolled down my cheek. "You know the answer."

"No I don't. I hope I know the answer, but I want to hear you say it. I have to hear you say it."

"Aram… Please…"

"Ash, tell the truth. Do you love me?"

"I do… There, are you happy?"

"Then why can't you be with me?"

"Because I'm going to marry William."

"You're not married yet, Ash. There's time. Leave him. Let's start over. We'll figure out the rest as we go. All I want is to be with you. Please? Leave him."

"And then what? Would you leave Kiley?"

"Yes. I'm serious. Let's do it in two weeks. We'll pack our stuff and move into a hotel until we can get an apartment. We won't tell anyone where we are. We'll just escape with each other. It's always been just us anyway." I looked at Aram and knew he meant it.

"We can't."

"God, why not?"

"I don't want to hurt everyone like that. We can't do it, Aram. It's too late."

"No it's not. It's not too late, Ash."

"Yes it is."

CHAPTER 38
DON'T LEAVE

Riley Adams

The sun hadn't shone all day. I watched the rain beat against the window as I looked out into the darkness while waiting on Aram to return home. I had no idea where he was. He had been disappearing a lot lately and that worried me so much I couldn't break my trance as I watched the raindrops gather on the glass. When I saw his headlights penetrating the blackness of the night as he parked his car in the parking lot, I prepared myself for the worst.

Aram opened the door and sighed as soon as he entered the apartment. He was drenched. I offered to get him some towels to dry off.

"No, I'm fine," he snapped back.

"Okay, I was just trying to help." He unbuttoned his shirt and tossed it to the linoleum in the entryway. He then kicked off his boots and walked to the bedroom. I walked over and picked his shirt up. It smelled somewhat funny, but I couldn't detect why. I grabbed a hanger from the closet and hung it in the bathroom to dry. Aram entered the bathroom and grabbed a towel. He didn't look at me.

"What's wrong?" I asked.

"Nothing is wrong. Why?"

"You appear upset."

"I'm not," he claimed.

"Well you look like you are."

"I don't know what to tell you, Kiley. I'm not upset. What do you want me to say?"

"You don't need to be a dick," I said.

"Whatever," he muttered under his breath as he walked away. I followed him.

"Where have you been?" I asked in a curt tone.

"Here we fucking go with the questions."

"Why are you being like this? It's a simple question that's justifiable. You disappear now and you never used to. I want to know where you go." I looked at him as I spoke. He busied himself with finding dry clothes.

"It's none of your business. I'm sick of having to explain myself every time I leave this goddamn apartment. It feels like a fucking prison. Have you ever considered that maybe I disappear just to fuck with you?"

"Why would you do that?" He continued fiddling with clothes in the closet. "For God's sake, would you quit fucking around in that closet and talk to me? Quit acting like a child!" I yelled finally.

"You act like my fucking mother. I have a mother, I don't need another one. Why don't you leave me alone?"

"I will when you answer my question."

"Fuck your question," he shouted. "I don't have to answer to you, or anyone else. I'm a fucking adult and can do as I please without persistent interrogations."

"You're a fucking liar and a coward," I said.

"How am I a liar and a coward?" He finally made eye contact.

"Because you're dodging the question and trying to make me look like the enemy here. You're a liar, Aram."

"Fuck you, Kiley. If you think I'm a liar, then so be it. I can't do anything about that. I'm not going to get sucked into another one of your attempts to control me though. Fuck that. I've had my fill of your goddamn rules and questions. Leave me alone."

"Fuck me? Fuck me? Is that what you say to someone you sup-posedly love? Are you listening to yourself? You sleep next to me. I do your laundry. I cook your meals. And all you can say is fuck me? I can't believe this… I mean, I really can't believe this at all," I said as I walked out of the room. I felt so angry I wanted to break something. I wanted to hit the wall or the mirror in the bathroom. I wanted to destroy something and pretend it was Aram's face.

Aram never followed me. He stayed in the bedroom and that only pissed me off more. I paced back and forth in the living room until I couldn't take it any longer. I stormed back into the bedroom to find Aram packing a bag.

"What the fuck is this?" I asked as I motioned toward his bag with my hand.

"What does it look like?"

"Fucking answer me!" I screamed.

"I'm leaving tonight. I can't take this shit," he said defiantly.

"You're leaving, huh? Where are you going? Who are you fucking, Aram? Be honest for once in your life. Who is the whore?"

"I'm not fucking anyone. You're delusional."

"Then where are you going? Fucking tell me!"

"I'm just going, Kiley. I don't want to be here."

"Where do you want to be?"

"Anywhere but here," he responded while he pushed a few more articles of clothing into his bag before zipping it closed. He looked up at me for a moment and then walked past me.

"Wait!" I yelled. "Aram!" He didn't respond. I was left standing in the bedroom like an idiot. Suddenly I was struck by such an extreme surge of panic that I felt lightheaded. "Aram!" I yelled again. Still nothing. I ran out of the bedroom frantically. No matter what, I loved him.

"Don't leave, Aram. Please, don't leave," I pleaded desperately. I knew it sounded pathetic, but I couldn't help it. I couldn't let him leave.

"Kiley, don't make this difficult," he said.

"Aram…" I started to cry, despite my best efforts to remain strong. "Please… I need you. Don't you know how much I love you? Do you know, Aram?" I asked between sobs.

"I have to leave."

"No you don't! Please, Aram. Please!"

"I think we may need a break."

"God, why? Please…"

"Kiley, don't cry. You know we haven't been getting along."

"I love you," I repeated as the tears streamed down my cheeks. "I love you, Aram!"

"I don't know what to say," he said stoically.

"You don't have to say anything. You love me, I know you do. You'll love me like I love you. Just give us time. You'll love me," is all I could say as he looked at me before he opened the door and stepped back into the rain.

CHAPTER 39
HELP!

Turner Brennan

I love the rain. I listened to the rhythmic sound as I piddled with a painting I would probably never finish. I took a pain pill about an hour before and I started to feel the rush of euphoria. It made everything feel extraordinary. I smiled to myself as I studied the messy canvas that would have stressed me out at any other time. One of my favorite songs played on my computer and I started a silly dance when I suddenly heard someone knock on the door.

I opened the door to see Aram standing there, wet from the rain.

"Oh my, come in!" I said as he stood in front of me, shaking the moisture from his shirt. "What are you doing here?"

Aram walked past me, noticeably upset. "I think it's over," he said simply.

"What's over?'

"I think I just broke up with Kiley."

"Oh no," I said convincingly. I felt my mood lift even more. I couldn't allow Aram to know that though. "What happened?" I asked, maintaining my contrived concern.

"I don't know. I can't take her anymore. It's too much." Aram looked around the apartment as he stood in the entranceway.

"Oops, you'll have to excuse my manners. Come in! Do you want something to drink?"

"What do you have?" he asked.

"I have wine and soda."

"Wine would be great," he replied in a flat tone.

"Coming right up," I said as I scampered into the kitchen, trying unsuccessfully to bottle my joy. The damn high I felt from the pill wasn't helping.

I uncorked the bottle of wine after a brief struggle. Aram stood in the entranceway. I could only imagine what was going through his mind as he waited on me. I wanted so badly to know what had happened with Kiley and if they were really over, but I couldn't come across as nosey. I had to let him tell me when he felt ready. I filled a tumbler with wine for Aram. I poured myself some as well, but only half a wine glass full since I still felt the numbness from the pain pill.

"Here you go," I said as calmly as I could as I handed Aram the glass full of wine. He took it from me and immediately took a drink. He didn't savor the taste at all. He simply gulped it down and then stared at his glass. I took a sip from my wine glass and felt the effects from the pain pill accelerate.

I made my way to the living room and Aram followed blindly behind me. He sat on the edge of my bed and took another long drink, almost finishing the wine. I knew I should sit down, but I couldn't. I was too excited.

"What is this?" Aram asked while motioning to the canvas I had been working on prior to his arrival.

"Oh my," I said self-consciously. "It's just something I was messing around with. I guess I was bored."

"I like it," he declared before finishing his drink. I stood in front of him. I glanced over my shoulder at the canvas and then back at Aram to gauge whether or not his sentiment was genuine. It was. I smiled. I wanted to run over to him and hug him tightly and kiss his cheek.

"Thank you," I said, feeling a bit bashful for some reason. "Do you want some more wine?"

I returned and handed Aram his second glass of wine. I had barely touched mine but I felt wonderful. I tried to remain serious, even though all I wanted to do was dance.

"So what happened?" I asked after an extended silence.

"I don't really know," he said. "She's just… She tries to control me and I hate it."

"What do you mean? She tells you what to do?" I asked, trying to keep him talking.

"No, she mostly just wants to know where I am at all times. It's like she wants me to fucking stay confined to the apartment like some pet. I can't take it anymore."

"I'm sorry," I said, surprised at how convincing I sounded.

"It's not your fault," he relayed.

"I know, but I still don't like to see you this upset. You don't deserve it."

"Thank you. That means a lot."

"I mean it, Aram. I can't imagine what she's thinking."

"Oh well. It's over."

"Do you still love her?" I asked, fearing his response.

"I don't think I ever did," he said.

"Well then it's probably for the best." I felt my stomach turn as adrenaline caused my hands to shake. I couldn't believe Aram's answer.

"Listen, I hate to bother you…" Aram began.

"You're not bothering me at all," I interrupted.

"I appreciate it, Turner. But I was going to ask you if I could stay here tonight." He looked up from his drink after he asked. I couldn't keep from smiling.

"You can stay here for as long as you want," I said, realizing my voice may have sounded way too cheerful.

"I don't know what I'm going to do, but I don't want to think about it tonight."

"Then don't. You'll stay here." I finished my wine and felt so alive I couldn't conceal my excitement any longer. I sat my wine glass on the desk next to the canvas and moved over to Aram. He didn't notice me at first, but as I approached, he looked up from his glass. I looked down, feeling sexier than I had ever felt before. His eyes remained fixed on mine. He slowly sat his glass on the floor beside the bed and that's when he stood up. We stood facing one another for a moment that felt absolutely perfect. I could feel the sexual tension pulling my body closer to his. His eyes revealed that he felt the same way. Without thinking, I leaned in to kiss him. As my lips touched his, I felt his hands grip my face and pull me near. His tongue entered my mouth and my mind blanked.

Making love with Aram was even more amazing than I had conceived in my most erotic fantasies. I lay underneath him breathing heavily as I ran my hand the length of his back, feeling my fingertips clinging to his sweaty skin. I heard my phone go off indicating someone had sent me a text. I had no idea what time it was, but it had to be getting late. My phone sounded again.

"Are you going to get that?" Aram finally asked, sounding a bit annoyed. He rolled off me and I hurriedly walked over to the desk to silence my phone before it sounded again. I pressed the button to reveal the message. It said, "I miss you," from Jakob. I stared at the screen. *Why did he have to text me at that exact moment?* I finally had everything I had ever wanted. As I deleted the message, I, for some reason, felt unfulfilled.

CHAPTER 40
SECOND THOUGHTS

Ashley Morrison

I stood in the garage watching William work to fix the front tire on my bike. It was hot outside and the sun shone brightly as perspiration gathered on his forehead. I wanted to take a bike ride to sort through whatever had happened in the parking lot when I met Aram, but now it was too hot. William insisted on fixing my tire, despite my claim that I no longer wanted to go for a ride. His arm muscles strained as he worked. I couldn't stop thinking about Aram. It made no sense as I watched William struggling in the afternoon heat. *Would Aram be so concerned about my flat tire?*

I knew I had everything most girls could ever want with William. He is a hard worker. He has a stable job. He has above average looks. Most importantly, he cares about me. Still, as I stood watching him wipe the sweat from his forehead with his hand, I felt like something was missing. Aram was the only thing on my mind and I didn't know why.

"I almost have it done," William said to me as I watched comfortably in the shade of the garage.

"I told you I don't need it done today," I said in the sweetest voice I could conjure.

"It's okay. I know you like to take your bike rides. I gotta keep you happy."

"Well, it's not necessary. I appreciate it, though."

When William finished, he requested I take the bike for a test run in the driveway. I think he wanted to prove to me that he had successfully helped, but it annoyed me more than anything. I eventually did take the ride and smiled as I rode past him and into the garage where I parked it and walked inside the house. He followed me indoors.

"Would you like something to drink?" I asked, feeling obligated to show concern since he had worked so hard to fix my bike.

"Yes, please."

"Water?"

"That would be great." He walked into the living room as I filled two glasses with water. I hate feeling domesticated.

I sat in the living room sipping my water as William watched some inane sitcom on television. He had seen every episode several times, but he still laughed like it was new. I wasn't sure if it was the heat or the persistent thoughts of Aram, but his laughter irritated me. I slouched in the chair, resting my glass on the arm as I stared at the screen like a zombie. That's how I felt. I felt like the living-dead, completely void of any emotion or passion. I had always aspired to have the middle class dream, and once it became actualized, I found it miserable. All the superficialities only obscured any real substance or meaning. I realized at that moment I hated my life. I hated what I had become.

"Do you want to go out for dinner tonight?" William asked, not diverting his eyes from his beloved show. "Doesn't Italian sound good?"

"Sure... I don't know... I don't care," I said from my stupor.

"Great. I'll get a shower after this show," William relayed, seemingly unaware of my answer.

"Okay," I said.

"Then we can rent a movie to watch. Won't it be nice to hang out here together?"

"Whatever." William's laughter drowned out my response.

"Can you believe that guy?" he asked, pointing at the screen. Even though I found myself staring at the screen, I had no clue what he was even talking about.

"Nope," I said.

"Ha-ha-ha. This fucking show..."

* * *

William talked on and on during dinner but I hadn't listened to one thing he said. I nodded my head periodically, but eventually I gave up on doing that. I just sat there, staring at my food as he alternated between his pasta and breadsticks.

"What's wrong with you tonight?" William finally asked after noticing I had not taken one bite of my ravioli.

"Nothing," I said while shuffling my food around on my plate with my fork, still unable to actually eat any of it.

"No, something is wrong. What is it?" he persisted.

"I don't know."

"Well you haven't touched your meal. I thought you wanted to go out?"

"You thought? Did I say I wanted to go out?"

"Yes you did."

"Ask yourself, William. Did I really affirm that I wanted to go out, or did you simply infer I did because you wanted to? What was my answer at the house when you asked the question?"

"Where is all of this coming from?"

"What was my answer? You don't know, do you? I didn't think so."

"Wow. I guess you're in a bad mood. Do you care to share why?"

"Never mind. It doesn't matter."

"It matters to me."

"Why does it matter to you?" I asked, feeling sick.

"Because I care about you," he replied without thinking.

"Why?"

"Because I love you, why else?" William never wavered.

"Are you sure?" I asked.

"Absolutely. Why do you question it?"

"I've been questioning everything lately," I divulged.

"What do you mean?"

"Exactly what I said."

"You are happy, aren't you?"

"Are you?" I asked.

"Of course I am." Hearing William's answer made me feel like it was too late for me to change my mind.

"Aren't you?" he eventually asked.

"I don't know," I finally revealed after an extended pause.

"Are you serious, Ashley? We're scheduled to get married in a little over a month."

"I know," is all I could say.

"What do you want to do?" he asked.

"I don't know," I repeated.

"I love you, Ashley. I love you with every part of me. I want you to love me too. I need you to love me entirely or not at all," he said, his full attention on me.

"I do love you," I finally said.

CHAPTER 41
THE END

Turner Brennan

I looked down at the sidewalk as I walked to meet Jakob on Sixteenth and Miller. I had no idea what I would say when I saw him. *How does one prepare for moments like this?* The bright sun created a picturesque scene. Flowers were in full bloom and had I not been so preoccupied with meeting Jakob, I would have stopped and knelt down beside the ceramic pots along the street in order to smell the blossoms. I felt guilty for not feeling worse than I actually did. I couldn't help my euphoria. Aram was finally mine.

I smiled as I thought of Aram. I covered my mouth with my right hand to conceal my joy. I must have appeared like an insane fool walking along aimlessly. Maybe I was a fool. I felt better than I ever had. I felt light enough to float away. I looked up at the full clouds overhead and laughed to myself. I felt like I was in a dream. I found myself drifting from the sidewalk to the grass and back to the sidewalk again while the breeze pushed my hair from my face. I was alive and did a little twirl right in the middle of the sidewalk to celebrate, uncaring as to who might see.

Jakob stood on the corner of Sixteenth and Miller in jeans, a worn t-shirt and black sunglasses. I could tell he was waiting on me because when he turned his head and noticed me walking down the sidewalk, he smiled. I approached, still feeling so good that any attempt to conceal my elation would have proven futile. I smiled as I walked toward him. I couldn't stop thinking about Aram.

"There you are," Jakob said as he leaned in to hug me. I hugged him back, not sure how to respond. "Where have you been? I've missed you," he continued.

"I'm sorry, I've been busy lately." I had quit smiling.

"You look beautiful. Come here. Damn, I've missed you." He hugged me again, this time holding me tightly against him as he took a deep breath.

"I've missed you too," I said dispassionately.

"Is something wrong?" he asked.

"No... I don't think so... Maybe."

"What is it?" His arms released me and I stood dumbly in front of him as he took his sunglasses off and looked into my eyes, trying to determine what was wrong with me.

"I don't know..." I couldn't tell him about Aram.

"Well, something is obviously wrong. You can tell me," he said in a calm voice. "I've missed you. I've missed us," he continued.

"I'm not sure we should continue this," I blurted, catching Jakob off guard.

"What?" he asked.

"I'm sorry," I said immediately.

"Why? I mean, what has happened? Did I do something wrong? I know I've texted you quite a bit. I apologize if I've come across as needy. Is that it? I've missed you, is all. I thought... I thought maybe you missed me too. I..."

"It's nothing you've done, Jakob. You're wonderful." I looked up at him to find his eyes fixed on mine. I could view the pain on his face. For the first time, I found myself forced to confront the potential I possessed to hurt another person. It felt terribly real. "It's just that,

I don't know if I'm ready for all of this. I guess I don't know what I want." I detested my inability to articulate what I was feeling. I felt like a coward. Maybe I was.

"I'm not trying to rush you, Turner. I hope you know that. I want whatever you want. I want to be around you as much as you are comfortable with. I don't want to push you away." Despite Jakob's sincerity, I couldn't help but feel chagrin for his attempts to appease me. It felt insincere and desperate. Aram would have never done or said anything he didn't feel.

"You've not done anything wrong. I'm just fucked up, or something."

"How are you fucked up?"

"Because you're wonderful and I'm not sure we should continue."

"But why?" he asked, unable to look away from me.

"I don't know."

CHAPTER 42
JUST ME

Kiley Adams

I found myself alone on the first warm evening of June. Aram had not returned, or even called. I knew he was angry with me, but I had hoped he would call me. God, how I needed to hear his voice. He had to know how devastated I was after he left. He had to know I'd do anything to get him back. I looked out the window at the surrounding darkness and felt as though it would creep inside my apartment and envelope me. Every time my phone chimed with a text, I would check it, hoping it was Aram, but it never was. I only felt more and more alone. I didn't know what to do.

I ran to the bathroom and knelt in front of the toilet. The wrenching stomach pain made me feel as though I would vomit at any moment, but all that came were dry heaves that made me lose my breath and feel light-headed. I could feel sweat collecting on my forehead. I wanted to die. It would have been easier.

I walked into the kitchen to pour a glass of water. I took a long drink and remembered I had not eaten all day. The very thought made me feel sick again. I walked back into the living room and sat on the couch, periodically sipping water as I stared out the window. *Maybe he knew.* I kept thinking the thought over and over. *Maybe somehow he knew.* I snapped out of it and concluded it was impossible. He had no idea I wasn't really pregnant. He had no reason not to believe me. That's what I found so troubling. Aram left, even though he believed I was carrying his child. *How could he do that?*

The more I thought about it, the more apparent it became that I should tell him that I wasn't pregnant. Of course, I wouldn't tell him I had never been pregnant. That would only push him farther away. Instead, I would tell him that I had a complication and hope that the realization that everything was back to the way it was before the pregnancy might bring him back to me. It had to. We had been happy until I freaked out and told him I was late. *What was I supposed to do?* Sure, it was foolish, but I felt desperate. I couldn't lose him.

I walked into the bedroom and picked up my favorite picture of Aram. I looked at his smile and traced his mouth with my fingertip. I took the picture outside of the library in Dublin, Ireland. He looked so happy in the picture that I framed it and kept it on my dresser so I was reminded of how happy he could be. I knew he could be that happy again with me. He had to give me another chance.

I picked up my phone and called him. I had to. I no longer cared about our argument or where he had been. All of that was meaningless now. All I cared about was hearing his voice, seeing his face and feeling his skin against mine. It rang once, twice, a third time and then I was sent to voicemail.

"Where are you, Aram," I said. "I miss you. Come home, baby." I waited for a moment, unsure if I was finished talking, and then hung up. I wondered what he was doing. I wondered where he was. I wondered if he was thinking of me.

I prepared a bath and sat down in the tub so that I could feel the warm water washing over my legs. I still felt sick, but the hot water numbed some of the pain enough that I could recline against the tub and slow my breathing a bit. I allowed my arms to be suspended in the water so that I could feel weightless. I always wondered how I would die. I think most people think about that, even if they never admit it. I always imagined I would die as an old woman after a lifetime of love and happiness. As I lay in the tub, I questioned whether that had been pure fantasy. I didn't want to die alone. I suppose no one wants to. I feared when I found myself unable to love anymore that I would end it. I didn't want to imagine myself as capable of suicide, but I had considered it an option. I don't know how else I would cope with the misery of being alone. Realistically, I would probably never be brave enough to go through with it.

I turned the water off and soaked in the tub as the steam ascended from the water's surface. I could never cut myself. I guess the only way I could foresee myself actually attempting suicide would be through an overdose. That way it would look like I simply went to sleep. That wouldn't be so bad. I could drift to sleep and never wake up. I could imagine the person who found me trying to wake me up and realizing that they couldn't. It sounded peaceful. I didn't think I could actually do it. I allowed my shoulders to relax enough that my head submerged underneath the water. I slowly emerged from the water, feeling the warmth trickle down my forehead and cheeks as I wiped my eyes with my hands so that I could open them. I wondered who would miss me. The only person I really wanted to miss me when I was gone was Aram. *Would he miss me?* I imagined that he'd be devastated. I envisioned him crying at my funeral. I could almost see him grieving, finding himself unable to cope with my absence. I smiled. I picked up my phone that I had positioned on top of my towel right beside the tub just in case he called. I looked at his name illuminated on my screen: Aram Young. God, I loved the man. I loved him so much. I texted him. "Would you miss me if I was gone?" I sent it and sat my phone on top of my towel again. I closed my eyes so that I could concentrate on how the warm water felt against my skin. Sometimes we take the smallest pleasures for granted.

CHAPTER 43
TOGETHER AT LAST

Turner Brennan

I woke up next to my love on Thursday. The breeze from the open window caressed my bare leg. I turned to face him. He was still sound asleep. I watched the white sheets decorated with faded red roses rise and fall as he breathed. I didn't want to move because I didn't want to wake him. It was the perfect moment. I wanted to freeze time and remain next to him in my bed forever. As I watched the breeze cause the curtain to sway, I noticed the flowers in the vase on the windowsill had wilted.

When I returned with my cup of coffee, Aram turned over and opened his eyes.

"Did I wake you?" I asked.

"No… What time is it?"

"Just after ten."

"Don't you have class today?"

"Nope," I said, smiling.

"How can you not have class?"

"I had something more important come up," I imparted, still smiling.

"What's that?"

"Spending time with you, silly." I took a sip of the coffee, which was still too warm for me to enjoy. "What about you, when do you have to work again?"

"Not until tomorrow."

"Great." I looked at Aram as he removed the sheet, revealing his naked body. God, he looked so good. I knew he could tell I was lusting for him, but I couldn't help staring. His abdomen muscles flexed as he turned over. His physique turned me on so much I could hardly contain myself. Aram folded his arm behind his head. He didn't at all appear self-conscious about being fully exposed to me, which was so sexy.

"What are you doing over there?" he finally asked. I snapped from my trance.

"Whatever do you mean?" I asked playfully.

"Ha-ha. You're funny." I looked at his abs again as he spoke. I looked lower until I saw what I truly wanted, what I ached for. I felt full of passion. I felt so alive. I wanted him. "Turner... Turner." My eyes lifted to meet his. "Why don't you come over here," he said while looking directly into my eyes. I moved toward him without saying a word.

"I need a shower," I told Aram after we made love. "I probably look hideous." I was still breathing heavily.

"You look beautiful, Turner. You know that, right?" I looked at Aram and smiled before I rolled over to get out of bed.

"Are you coming?" I asked, feeling Aram watching me as I walked to the bathroom.

"Not yet," he replied.

"Okay. I'll get in. You can join me when you're ready."

"That sounds good to me." I turned to walk away. "Turner, you need some flowers. Those are wilted," he said while looking at the vase on the windowsill.

"I kind of like them that way," I said.

* * *

I felt calm sitting on the patio at the small bistro on Fifteenth and Ohio as people walked by on the sidewalk. I finally was where I had wanted to be. I was next to Aram and took periodic sips from my Diet Coke as he peered at me through his black sunglasses. He smiled.

"You're so cute," he said. I didn't respond. I didn't want to ruin it by saying something sentimental and girly. Aram leaned back in his chair. He exuded confidence. I guess that's why I always imagined myself with an older man. He had an aura that made me feel safe and special. Just the way he moved made me want to give myself to him entirely. I would have right then if he would have asked me to.

"Do you mind if I drag you to an art store after lunch? I have to get some brushes," I asked as Aram took a bite from his club sandwich.

"I don't have any plans today," he relayed between bites.

"Perfect! I'm going to torture you then and make you look at all the goofy shit that makes me smile on the inside."

"Nothing would make me happier," he said. I wanted to hug him right then and squeeze him so that he knew I would never let him go.

Aram held my hand as we walked along the sidewalk. From time to time I'd skip as I forced his arm to sway in unison with mine. He laughed. At one point he stopped and plucked a flower from a bush.

"Here you go, pretty girl," he said in a formal tone.

"Why thank you, good sir," I replied. I held it in my free hand as we resumed our stroll. The sun shone overhead. I felt my blouse clinging to my skin. I was glad I wore a skirt, even though I hated showing my legs.

The air conditioned art store was a nice reprieve from the early summer heat. I walked from one exciting item to another, looking over my shoulder at Aram periodically to make sure he was still behind me. I found the brushes and pressed the bristles to my cheek to feel the softness. I must have looked foolish to Aram.

"I'll be over here," he finally said as I tested each brush.

"OK," I returned.

After I selected my brushes and a small print of a sleeping cat I decided I couldn't live without, I started looking for Aram. A brief panic seized me. *What if I had bored him? What if he left me?* My fears subsided when I saw him standing on the other end of the store.

"There you are, mister."

"Check this out," he said, pointing to an old photo booth.

"Does it still work?" I asked while inspecting it.

"Yeah. I asked the manager. Do you want to join me for a photo session?"

"Fuck yes I do!" Aram held the curtain to the side as I entered the booth and sat on the seat. He followed me in and sat beside me. He then put a dollar bill into the machine and waited.

"What are we supposed to do?" he asked.

"I have no idea," I replied. Just then a series of beeps sounded and then the machine snapped our picture. Neither of us was ready. We burst into laughter until the next series of beeps sounded.

"Smile," Aram said just before the picture was snapped. "For the last one, make a stupid face." I waited and when the beeps started again, I crossed my eyes and stuck my tongue out the side of my mouth. Just as the picture was taken, I felt Aram's lips on my cheek. I felt my face flush as we waited for the pictures to print. Aram handed me the three black and white photographs. We looked at them while sitting in the booth. With the pictures still clutched in my hand, I leaned over and kissed Aram. I felt him kiss me back as his hand massaged my thigh. I felt his hand move under my skirt. My breath escaped involuntarily before he pulled his hand away. He looked at me with piercing eyes. I was his and he knew it.

CHAPTER 44
RUNNING AWAY

Ashley Morrison

"I want to run away with you," I said as we walked along the railroad tracks. The tracks used to be our meeting place years ago. We'd walk and talk about our future. Maybe it was the sight of those tracks snaking into the horizon that always made our plans seem plausible. Aram walked beside me as I balanced on the rail before tottering over and landing back on the ground.

"Why do you say that, Ash?" Aram asked as he walked beside me.

"I don't know. I just feel like I should. I feel like it's the only solution to whatever has become of everything. I don't know who I am any longer. I feel like a stranger to myself. I don't feel alive," I said.

"Ash, you know I'd run away with you right now if that's what you wanted. But will that fix you?"

"I don't know. I don't know anything anymore. We should do it."

"I moved out," he said.

"What?"

"I left Kiley."

"Are you serious?"

"Yes…"

"I can't... I can't believe you actually left her," I said. I stopped walking and turned to face Aram.

"I told you I was serious about this."

"Where are you staying now?" I asked, curious if Aram had a plan at all.

"I'm staying with a friend for now. I've been waiting on you," he confessed.

"I can't believe this," I said, still in shock.

"Well believe it. We only get one life to live. I'm determined not to have any regrets."

"I wish I had your courage," I said.

"Just leave him, Ash. I don't know why you feel compelled to live a life you don't want any part of. Is it your mother? Are you doing this for her?"

"No, why would you say that?"

"I know how she tries to convince you that you need to get married and have children."

"What's wrong with that?" I asked.

"Nothing is wrong with that. What's wrong is feeling pressured to meet milestones without any passion."

"You don't know what you're talking about." I started walking again, though I wasn't sure why.

"You want to escape, don't you?"

"I don't know... Maybe... Is that wrong?" I asked, unsure of everything.

"It's not wrong if it's what you truly want. Is it what you really want?"

"I don't know."

"Ash, will you stop walking for a second and look at me?" I stopped and turned to face him. "You know how I feel. You know I want to be with you. If you want to go, let's get on a train and go. All we need is each other. We'll make everything else work in time."

"I'm getting married in a month."

"Would you stop with that excuse? You can call it off. Your mother will come around. Everything will be fine in time."

"I don't know…"

"Quit saying that," he commanded. "You're scared of being happy. You're scared of love. You're scared of living."

"I know… I feel like I should leave with you. I can't pinpoint why I feel that way, but it's what I feel. Part of me thinks it's just immature apprehension. I know I hate responsibility and feeling trapped."

"You should never feel trapped."

"I know… I just… What should I do?" I asked, feeling desperate.

"You should do what you want to do. You should do what will make you happy. You should disregard everything else and do what you feel," he said.

"I want to escape."

"Then you can. I love you and want to be with you. You love me, right?" he asked.

"You know the answer," I replied.

"You can never say it. No one else is around." He walked away from me and stopped with his back to me. "I love Ashley Morrison!" he yelled as loud as he could. A faint echo resounded.

"Oh my God, what are you doing?"

"I'm showing you how easy it is to admit your feelings."

"Aram!"

"Try it. It's liberating."

"I can't," I said bashfully.

"Are you scared to love me? Are you scared of love?" he prodded. I felt like I might cry. I started walking along the tracks again. Aram stayed behind for a moment and then jogged to catch up. "Are you scared of love, Ash?" I stopped walking.

"I'm not scared of love, Aram," I said while looking up at him. I felt my eyes tearing up. "It's not that I'm scared that I wouldn't be happy with you. I wish you wouldn't say that. That's not it at all. I want to love. I want to be happy. I want to feel alive. What scares me is what comes after that? What is next? What happens when there's nothing left to hope for?"

CHAPTER 45
LOVE ME

Kiley Adams

"So how have you been?" Ryan's emotionless voice asked as I sipped from the glass of water he provided. I don't know why, but I felt compelled to see him.

"I've been better," I replied. I found myself staring at his body. He was wearing a gray shirt that hugged his chest perfectly. His jeans had holes in both knees and hung just low enough that I could see the waistband of his red boxer briefs. I wondered who his last lover had been. *Did she have any feelings for him?*

"I'm sorry to hear that," he said. I don't know why I provided such a vague response. I knew damn well Ryan wouldn't ask me to elaborate about what was wrong. He really didn't care. *Why had I bothered to visit?*

"It's not your fault," is all I could think to impart. Ryan sat down in a chair next to the window in his living room. He glanced outside and then looked back at me. I didn't know what to say. I was lonely. I really just wanted to be around him. I moved closer and looked out the same window. Ryan's aloof demeanor only made me want him more. God, I felt so pathetic, but I wanted him to take me like he used to when he'd pull my hair and when I'd start to scream, he'd cover my mouth with his cupped hand. Those were the moments when I felt the most alive.

"How have you been?" I finally asked. In the throes of my fantasy I had forgotten my manners.

"I've been well," he said simply. I touched his arm. He didn't pull away. My fingertips touched his bicep and slowly moved underneath his shirt before I pulled my touch from him. Ryan remained unmoved.

"Is there anything new with you?" I asked, remembering why Ryan and I rarely talked when we were together years ago.

"Do you care?" he asked.

"Why would I have asked otherwise?" Ryan didn't answer. He simply stood up and moved closer to me. I froze. I stared right into his unblinking eyes. I felt his hand in the small of my back as he brought my body into his.

"Isn't this what you want?" he asked. His lips were inches from mine.

"I…" I couldn't catch my breath. His other hand worked to the back of my head. I could feel him grabbing a handful of my hair before he pulled my head backward.

"Answer me. Is this what you want?" he repeated.

"Yes…" is all I could whisper back.

* * *

"Ryan, I don't know what to do," I said. We were lying on the floor. My head rested on his arm. I moved so that I could look up at him as I spoke. He stared at the ceiling.

"Did you break up with Aram?" he asked after a pause.

"No… Well, I don't know. I guess you could say that."

"Then what's there to consider?"

"I don't know if it's over. I don't know what I want."

"That doesn't make any sense to me," he said.

"Why do you say that?"

"What is so goddamn confusing about all of this? If you're not with him, it's over. It's that simple. Move on. I don't understand everyone's preoccupation with the past."

"It happens when you care," I blurted.

"I suppose," he said, followed by a long silence.

"Does anyone actually love who they are with?" I asked. "Are relationships nothing more than convenience?"

"I don't know. I don't think anyone knows. What does it matter?"

"Love doesn't matter?"

"I don't know. Does it?"

"God, you're so cold." I moved my head so I was no longer resting on his arm. I couldn't stand Ryan most of the time. I faced away from him. I didn't want to cry in front of him.

"What's the matter with you?"

"Nothing," I said.

"Jesus, are you getting all emotional on me?"

"No."

"Listen, you need to figure out what you want and go after it. It's that simple. But the moping and self-loathing is unbecoming."

"I'm fucking sorry for being sad, Ryan. Not everyone can make it through life feeling nothing."

"I have feelings, Kiley."

"You could've fooled me."

"Don't be like this."

"Be like what?" I almost yelled.

"Like this. Don't act like the world is coming to an end and you're the only one left to endure the misery. Everyone's miserable. Deal with it!"

"That's a great way to live life, Ryan. What do you want out of life?"

"Nothing."

"Do you mean that?"

"I suppose I do."

"That makes me sad," I confessed.

"Well, it shouldn't."

"Am I really that bad?" I asked. I knew Ryan would tell me the truth.

"No. Who said you were?"

"No one. I just... I don't know. I feel worthless sometimes."

"You shouldn't feel that way," Ryan said in a calming voice. It was the first hint of emotion he had displayed since I arrived.

"Well I do. But thank you. Would you ever want me? I mean, would you ever consider getting back together if we could figure everything out?"

"Are you serious, Kiley?" he asked, looking over at me as I looked at the ceiling.

"I don't know. Would you want me?" I asked again.

"Kiley..." he began, before I interrupted.

"Just answer me, Ryan. All bullshit aside, would you want me?" He looked away for a moment and then looked back at me.

"I have a girlfriend," he said.

CHAPTER 46
DOCTOR'S APPOINTMENT

Turner Brennan

I hate waiting rooms. There's something unsettling about the sterile smell and the absolute silence. The only noise was the lame music being played to ease everyone's anxiety. Periodically the older man beside me would cough, interrupting the stream of monotony. I just wanted to feel better. I had vomited the last two mornings and felt queasy the rest of the day. Aram tried to help me, but I couldn't pinpoint what was wrong. Initially I thought it was the flu, but I never developed a substantial fever. Aram pestered me until I agreed to get an appointment to get some medicine. I felt bad. Not only because I was sick, but because I didn't have the energy to enjoy Aram's company. That's always how it goes.

"Turner Brennan," the voice said. I looked up to notice a middle-aged nurse calling my name from the doorway. She held a clipboard in her hand.

"That's me," I announced. The older man beside me looked disgusted that my name was called before his. I smiled at him.

"Right this way," the nurse instructed.

Once I was seated on the examining table with my feet dangling, the nurse told me she would be right back and shut the door. I looked around at the various anatomy posters on the wall. I wanted to steal one for my apartment, but decided against it. *Why did I have those impulses?*

"Turner Brennan?" the nurse's voice asked from behind the closed door.

"Yes," I replied. The nurse opened the door and walked inside the examination room.

"I'm going to get your vitals and take your temperature," she said as she retrieved her stethoscope from around her neck. "Then I'm going to ask that you take this cup and provide a urine sample." She handed me a clear plastic cup with a lid. I held the cup in my hands as she listened to my chest, side, and back with her stethoscope.

"What do you think I have?" I asked as she prepared to take my blood pressure.

"I'll let the doctor speak to you in a bit. I'm sure we'll have you feeling better in no time," she assured. Some nurses have the kindest disposition.

After I provided the urine sample, I sat on the same examination table and waited for the doctor. I felt like a trapped animal. The boring music only made me more anxious. I felt a hot flash and then feared that my palms would be sweaty when the doctor arrived. *What would happen if he or she wanted to shake my hand?*

A knock came and was followed by the doctor cracking the door. "Miss Turner Brennan?" the doctor asked.

"Yes," I answered as the doctor entered the room and shut the door behind her.

"Hello, I'm Dr. Angelo," she said as she smiled. Luckily she didn't extend a hand for me to shake.

"Nice to meet you," I said.

"So you've been feeling pretty lousy the last few days?"

"Yeah, and I can't figure out what the issue is. I've mostly been dealing with nausea and fatigue."

"Turner, you're pregnant." Dr. Angelo's voice didn't waver. I stared at her without blinking.

"Are you sure?" I asked, not sure how else to respond.

"Yes. I suspected pregnancy, that's why I wanted a urine sample. Are you okay?" she asked.

"Of course," I replied, feeling like I would faint at any moment.

"There are a number of options for you to consider if this is an unwanted pregnancy. However, it is important that the father be notified so that he can be involved in the decision-making process." Her words flowed with such ease I would have sworn she was reading from a brochure if I were not seated right in front of her.

"Father?"

"Yes, you need to notify the father of the child," Dr. Angelo repeated.

"Oh, yes, of course. I'm sorry… it's just that… Well, I wasn't expecting this," I confessed.

"I know this can be a stressful time in a woman's life, but there is plenty of information and support available, no matter your personal situation. I've instructed the nurse to provide you with informational pamphlets before you leave today. Do you have any questions for me?" she asked while smiling at me.

"Not that I can think of," I said.

"OK. Well, you can make your way to the front desk for those pamphlets. You'll want to set your next appointment in the next week or so to ensure we get you on a routine schedule."

"Next appointment?" I asked, feeling as if my brain had stopped working.

"Yes, you'll need to schedule regular appointments from this moment until the birth of the child, unless you decide to terminate the pregnancy."

"I don't think abortion is an option," I said. I wasn't sure why I had said that.

"Then you'll need to schedule additional appointments so that we can track your pregnancy and make sure everything is going well." I could tell she was ready to move on to her next client. *Couldn't she tell I was about to collapse? Wasn't it evident that my life had ended?*

"OK, I'm sorry. I'm not thinking."

"It's quite all right. You will want to contact the father in order to include him during this process."

"I will," I said. *Who was the father?*

"Remember, you have options, Turner. Call the office if you need anything else. I'll look forward to seeing you soon." Dr. Angelo then opened the door and left. The door remained open and I sat frozen on the examination table for a moment as people walked by. I felt a loneliness I had never felt before while sitting in that room watching the people walking past as if I wasn't there at all. I didn't know who the father was. I didn't know how to tell Aram. I didn't know how to tell my parents. I didn't know anything.

CHAPTER 47
LUNCH WITH MOTHER

Ashley Morrison

"Ash, what is going on with you?" my mother asked as we sat at the Italian restaurant waiting on our pasta dishes to arrive. I pushed my salad around with my fork before I looked up to respond.

"What do you mean?" I asked in an effort to determine her intentions.

"You know you're worrying William, right? He's all upset. He thinks that you might back out of the wedding."

"What? How do you know that?"

"He told me when I called yesterday to speak to you. He told me you haven't been yourself lately."

"Jesus, mother."

"Don't give me that, Ashley. What's going on with you? You're not actually considering…"

"Considering what? Say it, mother. What am I not possibly considering?"

"Stop it, Ashley. I don't understand this hostility. What's wrong with you?"

"I don't know."

"There has to be something that's caused you to be this upset. Aren't you still happy with William?"

"William is fine," I replied in a vague manner.

"Then what is it?"

"It's... I don't know... I... Sometimes, I don't think I should marry William. It has nothing to do with him. He's always been great to me. It has to do with me, I suppose, and where I see myself."

"Ash, what the hell are you talking about? You realize you're not a child any longer, right? You understand that this isn't a minor commitment you've made. This is a life decision. Your decisions don't only impact you any longer. They impact quite a few people."

"I know... Why do you always do this?"

"Do what?" she asked.

"Try to make me feel guilty. Don't you think I wish I was normal? Don't you think I want to get married and live happily-ever-after? Why would I punish myself?"

"You're not punishing yourself, Ashley. You're punishing everyone else."

"There you go again. Isn't this my life? Shouldn't my happiness count?"

"Your happiness does count, Ash. That's why marrying William is the right thing to do. He loves you. He wants you to be the mother of his children. He has a good job and is stable."

"Stable? What does that even mean?" I asked, feeling so irritated that I didn't care that I raised my voice.

"He's not like that other guy you dated."

"Aram?"

"Yes..."

"What did you have against Aram?"

"He wasn't the one for you. He was..."

"Say it, mother. What?"

"He was way too impulsive. A guy like that will never settle down. I'm sure the passion was nice to experience, but trust me when I say that romance like that never materializes into a long-term commitment."

"Why is that?" I asked.

"That's not what marriage is. Marriage is stability. Marriage is every day."

"And what is romance?"

"Romance?"

"Love like I experienced with Aram," I said, knowing she didn't want to answer the question.

"What you had with Aram was not love," she said flatly.

"What was it?"

"Infatuation. It was only infatuation."

"You're wrong. You're so damn wrong."

"Ashley! Watch your mouth."

"Don't give me that. You can call a three-year relationship I had an infatuation but I can't say the word damn?"

"Ashley, you're not thinking about your future. You're only thinking about what you want right now."

"Isn't that what I should be thinking about? Isn't that what's most important?"

"No. Your future is what should be most important. Your future you are building with William should be your preoccupation, not these silly musings about ex-boyfriends."

"They're not silly to me."

"Well, they're silly, nonetheless."

Our meals arrived, which stifled our argument momentarily. I hadn't taken a bite from my salad. I picked up my other fork and dug into the pasta so that I could watch the steam rise. I remembered a day when that would have made me smile. My mother ate her pasta as if nothing was wrong. That was always her way to deal with anything she deemed too distressing. She would simply act as if nothing had happened and somehow everyone in our family would forget the whole episode.

"You know it's too late to back out, don't you?" she finally said.

"What?" I asked, shocked that she had the audacity to persist with the topic.

"You have a dress already. The invitations have been mailed. It's too late to change your mind, Ashley. You made a commitment. Now you have to see it through."

"Goddamn, you don't get it, do you? Does anyone give a damn what I want? Does anyone give a shit whether I want to get married or not?"

"Of course we care, Ashley. We love you. I love you. I only tell you this because I know you would regret not going through with this wedding. It's what is best for your future."

"Fuck the future!"

"Ashley!"

"I'm tired of thinking about all of this. I'm tired of planning my entire life. I'm tired of thinking about invitations and attire. I'm sick of dwelling on shit I don't really care about."

"What are you suggesting?" she asked. I could see the fear in her eyes. She knew she was losing control.

"I'm suggesting that I'll do what I want. I'd hope that you and everyone else will support me, no matter what."

"Ashley, I can't allow you to throw your life away."

"I'm hardly throwing my life away, mother."

"What would you call what you're doing? Are you even listening to yourself? Don't you hear how selfish you're being?"

"I suppose that I do," I said defiantly.

"I don't know what to do with you. I raised you to do what is right."

"I am doing what is right."

"What about William?"

"What about him?" I asked.

"He is what is best for you, Ashley."

"Is he?"

CHAPTER 48
SUNDAY DINNER

Kiley Adams

"Where's Aram?" my mom asked as she finished filling her glass with wine. I looked down at my plate. I wasn't sure what was in front of me. Ever since my mom became a vegetarian, I never knew what she fed me.

"What is this?" I asked while staring at it.

"Don't worry, you'll like it. Are you avoiding my question?"

"No, what did you ask?"

"Where's Aram," she repeated.

"Oh, sorry, I guess I'm a bit out of it. He had some work to do." I lied. I had no idea where Aram had been, or who he was even living with, but I couldn't tell my mom that. I didn't want to admit it to myself, let alone her.

"I sure hope he proposes to you soon," my mom said before she took a sip of her wine.

"Mom!"

"What? He's a great guy. You better hang on to him."

"I know he's great," I said while looking at my food. I no longer felt hungry.

"I'm serious. He's the perfect guy," she continued.

"Mom, I know how great Aram is. He is my boyfriend, remember?"

"Ha-ha, yes, of course. I'm sorry, it's just…"

"I know, you think he's hot."

"Kiley!"

"What, mom? It's true, isn't it?"

"I would never word it that way," she said. My mom drank the rest of her wine and filled her glass again before continuing. "He's very charming."

"He can be."

"Do you think he'll propose to you this year?"

"I don't think he's going to propose anytime soon," I relayed.

"Why is that? Aren't you two getting along?" she persisted.

"We're getting along. We have our arguments like anybody else, but we work through them."

"I hope so." She didn't know when to stop.

"He's fine. We're fine. Don't worry so much and whatever you do, never mention this to Aram. He'd freak out!"

"Oh, Kiley, I would never…Why would he freak out?"

"Mom, can't we talk about something else?"

"Why would he freak out?"

"I don't think he's ready for that type of commitment. I don't know if he's the type of guy to ever want to get married."

"Men don't ever want to get married. You have to convince them. You have to show them what they will be missing if they let you go. You have to make it impossible for them to envision a life without you," she said.

"I guess you're right."

"I know I am."

"Do you have any prospects?" I asked, trying to change the subject.

"Oh, no you don't, Kiley. We're not talking about me. We're talking about you."

"I know, but I don't want to talk about me." I smiled nervously after I spoke.

"You have to remember that guys don't think like girls." I felt myself wanting to get sick as my mom spoke. "They have different...well, interests," she said.

"I know about the birds and the bees, mom."

"It's not just that. You have to remember that if you keep your man happy, he won't stray. Do you know what I mean?"

"I believe so," I said in a disgusted voice.

"I'm serious, Kiley. You have to concern yourself with those needs."

"I don't think that's all a relationship consists of," I said.

"Well, of course not. But, it's a crucial element. You have to keep the guy interested. That means you have to remain interesting to him."

"I'll buy some lingerie," I joked. My mom had no idea how inadequate she made me feel at times.

"Men get bored easily. They have short attention spans."

"Now I know that is true!"

"So they need reminded on a regular basis where their love resides. Love, for a man, is transient."

I finished my wine and poured another glass. If I had to listen to my mom's theories, I should at least be allowed to get drunk.

"Are you going to eat that?" Her question snapped me back into reality.

"I don't know, I'm still unsure what it is," I replied.

"Do you want me to fix you something different?"

"No, I'm just not very hungry tonight."

"Kiley, don't worry so much. Everything will work out," my mom said randomly.

"OK...thanks."

"You're acting so distracted tonight. I don't know what it is, but something is on your mind."

"I'll be fine."

"I know. I just don't like to see you like this."

"Like what?" I had tried my best to act as though nothing was wrong.

"Distant. It'll be fine, though. When you get home, spend a little time with Aram. You should enjoy being young. It won't last forever."

"Nothing does," I replied.

"That's very true, Kiley. Would you like me to open another bottle of wine?" she asked after she had already stood up to do so.

"Sure," I said as she walked past my chair on her way to the kitchen.

I stared out the large window while my mom retrieved the cork-screw and a new bottle of wine. I could hear the clanking of the bottle every time it made contact with the counter as my mom struggled to remove the cork. I couldn't tell my mom the truth. She wouldn't understand. It was likely she'd take Aram's side anyway. I didn't know what to do, but I knew I couldn't lose Aram. He was the one I had to marry. Maybe my mom knew what she was talking about. Maybe it was up to me to save our relationship. When she returned with the bottle, I noticed her glass was already half empty. She must have taken a drink while in the kitchen. I waited until she filled my glass and then raised it to her as she sat down in her chair across from me. I wanted her to know I would never give up. I would not lose Aram.

CHAPTER 49
MEETING WITH MINISTER BOB

Ashley Morrison

I didn't want to be there. But, for whatever reason, I found myself seated in Minister Bob's office next to William. I felt detached from everything and everyone. I thought incessantly about fleeing with Aram, but whenever he would try to get me to actually do it, I would say it was impossible. *What kind of name is Bob for a minister?* It made him sound like a fucking moron. I hoped he knew that. I wanted to tell him just to make sure. I smiled as I thought of doing so. I could imagine how his face would deflate and how his moral pretension would never recover.

"Where is he?" I asked William as I checked the time on my cell phone.

"I'm sure he'll be here shortly," William answered. William was too nice. Aram would have grabbed me by the hand and stormed out of the office five minutes ago. In a fit of passion, I could imagine him asking me to elope in Vegas instead. I missed that spontaneity. *Isn't it human nature to find fault with what we have?*

"I sincerely apologize for the wait," Minister Bob began. "It's been one of those days." He took a deep breath to collect himself as soon as he entered the office. "How are you two today?" he asked. I cringed.

"We're doing well, thank you," William said. I smiled and didn't say anything.

"Well, shall we get started? See, we were set to do the couple questionnaire today, if I'm not mistaken," he said.

"Yes, that's correct," William replied.

"Great... How are the plans coming?" Bob asked the question while he dug in his desk drawers for the questionnaires. His apparent ineptitude disgusted me.

"You'll have to ask Ashley about that," William said, followed by a chuckle.

"Smart man," Bob answered. Their discourse sounded pathetically contrived. Bob stared at me after he spoke, as if he expected me to answer while he tried to locate the goddamn questionnaire papers.

"It's been a long process," I stated as cordially as I could. I wanted to tell him what I really thought. I wanted to tell him that marriage was a sham, that it was merely a formality for everyone else's benefit. I felt a surge of adrenaline. *Did anyone understand that all of the preoccupation with the attire, decorations, and invitations had absolutely nothing to do with love?* I felt alone. Everyone else appeared content. Every person I talked to was happy for me.

"That's probably a fair statement," Bob said. I quit listening after that and instead sat in the chair smiling dumbly. I figured that was what everyone expected.

Bob handed the questionnaires to us and instructed that we part our chairs to take the damn personality test so that we wouldn't look at each other's answers. I refused to move my chair and instead acted like I didn't hear him. Bob stared at both of us until William finally moved his chair away from mine. I just smiled. When he told us to start, I began by reading the question and then choosing the most appropriate answer. Then I considered how fucking stupid the whole process was and quit reading the questions. I doodled on the side of the answer book instead. I checked my phone for messages. I looked around Bob's office. I noticed a picture of his family behind his desk. He had his arm around his wife and their two boys were standing in front of them. Everyone was smiling. I wondered if their joy was genuine. I snapped from my reveries and filled the answer bubbles in haphazardly. I didn't care any longer. The world felt fake.

"Are you both done?" Bob asked. I extended my packet to him. "Oh no, we're going to go through this together. You're going to score your own sheet and then we'll gauge the compatibility issues. Don't worry, everyone has some compatibility deficiencies. It's perfectly natural. That's what we want to do. We want to locate the areas where there may be some conflict and discuss those issues here so that we can be proactive." I never heard anyone refer to proactive measures when discussing marriage. He was truly an idiot.

"So there are only a few issues that you will want to discuss before our next meeting," Bob began. "Our next meeting will be our final one before the wedding rehearsal. You're almost there, can you believe it?"

"It's gone by quickly," I said.

"Ashley, you know that you will learn to cherish William's predictability. It's an admirable trait. And William, you'll learn to cherish Ashley's impulsiveness. Sometimes opposite traits in partners allow for a more functional cooperative approach. That's the beauty of a partnership. I can tell you this after working with you two for a few months: you will complement each other nicely."

"Thank you," William said. "I'm always open to compromise. I know that will be the key to making our marriage work."

"William, you're so right. Compromise is paramount. You will have arguments. Some of them will be about serious matters. Others will be about trivial matters. What is important to remember in those times is that your love will outlast those incidents. As long as you both continue to work on your relationship, your love will always be in blossom."

I stared at Minister Bob as he spoke, not because I was listening intently to what he was saying, but because I was trying to ascertain how to know what love is. Sometimes I thought I knew, but then I would hear some superficial explanation like what Bob continued to espouse and that would force me to confront the idea that perhaps all notions of love are only fabrications perpetuated by those who are afraid to be alone. *I don't want to be alone, so does that mean I love William?*

"Do either of you have any other concerns you'd like to talk about today? We have a few minutes left." William looked over at me after Bob asked. I looked back at him.

"No, I don't think so," William imparted. William stood to shake Minister Bob's hand and I did the same. As I opened the door to leave the office, I felt William's hand in the small of my back and knew I would marry him.

CHAPTER 50
NO ONE UNDERSTANDS

Turner Brennan

Jakob kept calling and leaving sad voicemails about how he missed me. His messages revealed details about his new paintings and about some quirky button he purchased that he now wears on his lapel. I listened to them and then deleted them. His voice made me feel terrible. I hated causing others to hurt. I guess it's inevitable.

Aram still wasn't home. He hadn't been home on time all week. I took a drink from my decaffeinated tea and almost spit it out. It tasted horrible. I wanted a strong cup of coffee so badly, but I decided to give up caffeine during my pregnancy. It still felt so unreal to think of myself as pregnant. I sat my mug of tea on the windowsill and lifted my shirt so that my stomach was exposed. I looked at it and then ran my right hand over my skin, feeling the tightness of my muscles. I knew my body would never be the same. There was a life inside me now, growing every day. *Why do I feel lifeless?*

Aram walked inside the apartment as if he wasn't an hour late. I didn't say anything. I didn't have the energy to argue with him. I found myself still struggling with how to tell him I was pregnant.

"Do we have anything for dinner? I'm starved," Aram said as he took his shoes off.

"I'll make you something," I said as I stood up.

"You don't have to, Turner. I can find something."

"No, I want to make something for you."

"Hey, come here," Aram said as he grabbed my upper arm. "Are you going to walk right by me without giving me a hug?"

"I'm sorry. I'm kind of out of it," I admitted.

"Is something wrong?" Aram asked.

"Is grilled cheese and asparagus okay? I haven't gone to the store yet."

I watched Aram eat the sandwich I made him. He looked so handsome with his shirt unbuttoned. Aram's tan skin turned me on so much. His brown eyes looked up from his plate at me. I swear he could tell what I was thinking. He smiled at me. I put a finger to my lips and bit my fingernail, unable to disguise my desire. He took a drink from his Diet Coke and then wiped his mouth with his napkin. Aram stood up and moved toward me. I froze in my chair and could only watch him as he approached. He extended his hand toward me. I grasped it and he gently guided me from my seat. When I was standing in front of him, he placed his right arm around my waist and brought my body into his. I took a deep breath. I loved how Aram smelled. He held me tightly and I rested my head on his shoulder.

"I never want this to end," I whispered.

"Me either," he said. I leaned back so that I could look up at him. He looked down at me. I rested my head on his shoulder again. I felt him squeeze me. "Let's go," he said finally. He broke from me and led me to the bedroom.

I struggled to catch my breath after it was over. Sweat dripped from Aram's chin onto my chest. I kept my legs around him. Eventually he broke from me and lay beside me.

"You're amazing," he said aloud as he wiped the sweat from his forehead with his hand. My hair was wet from the perspiration.

"So are you," I said.

"Are you okay?" Aram asked. He turned his head to look at me after I didn't respond right away.

"Yes, I'm fine."

"You don't sound fine."

"I am, it's just…"

"Are you still feeling sick?" Aram asked.

"A little. I think I'm getting better, though."

"Did you get medicine?"

"I don't need any," I divulged.

"Well that's good. Is it just the flu then?"

"I…" I stopped before the lie came out of my mouth. "Where have you been all week?"

"What do you mean?"

"You haven't been home on time all week."

"Oh, I haven't noticed. I guess I've been putting in a little extra time at the job. I should be free this weekend though."

"Okay," I said, not believing him.

"You're so beautiful," Aram said while still looking at me. "I love your body."

"Is that all that you love?" I asked.

"What?"

"Nevermind."

"Where did that come from?" he asked.

"I don't know. I'm tired."

"I hope you start feeling better. Can I get you anything?"

"No. I'll be fine."

"Do you want to go out this weekend?" he asked. I felt nauseous just thinking about going out to a restaurant. "Are you okay?" I sprang from the bed and ran to the bathroom. I knelt in front of the toilet. After dry heaving a few times, my stomach felt a bit more settled.

"Do I need to take you to the emergency room?" Aram asked as he stood in the doorway.

"No, it won't do any good," I said.

"I don't understand."

"Don't worry about it, Aram. I'm going to be fine."

"You don't look like it."

"I don't want you to see me like this."

"Turner, it's you. You don't have to be embarrassed around me."

"I just…" I gagged again and spit some bile into the toilet. "Get out, please."

"I want to help you," he said.

"You can't help me, Aram."

CHAPTER 51
BAD NEWS

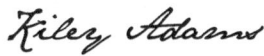

The faucet dripped all day and all night. I tried to fix it, but it still dripped. I could hear it from the living room. I was forced to listen to it because I didn't have the energy to leave the apartment. It had been over a week since I saw Aram. The air conditioner hadn't turned off in over an hour. It must have been really hot outside. Just then there was a knock on the door. I didn't get up. There was another knock. God, I didn't want to talk to anyone. A third knock sounded.

Aram stood before me when I opened the door. I couldn't speak. Instead I stood in the doorway staring at him like an imbecile.

"Can I come inside, Kiley?" he asked.

"Yeah," I said, still shocked that it was him. He walked past me and stood in my living room fanning his face with his hand. I eyed him. His t-shirt was wet from sweat and his shorts were wrinkled. His skin appeared darker than I had remembered.

"Where have you been?" I said after I closed the door.

"That's not relevant," he answered.

"You're right," I conceded. "I don't care. I'm so happy you're here." I walked over to him and hugged him. He hugged me back with one arm. "Are you going to stay?" I asked as I stepped back from him.

"Not now," he said in an emotionless tone.

"Are you coming back soon?"

"Maybe."

"Is there anything I can do?" I asked.

"No," he said.

"Would you like a drink?"

"I'll take some water."

"No problem. I'll be right back." I walked into the kitchen to pour Aram a glass of water. "You look good," I yelled from the kitchen. I didn't think I would have the courage to say that to him if I were standing in his view.

"Thank you. You look great too," he said as I entered the living room holding his glass of water. He took a drink as soon as I handed the glass to him. "Damn, it's so hot outside."

"I thought about going to the pool, but I don't have the energy."

"The pool would be nice." He took another drink after he spoke.

"I'm glad you visited," I said. "Aram, I need to tell you something."

"Go ahead." He sat his glass down on the coffee table beside the couch.

"I don't know how to say it," I confessed.

"Just say it."

"I lost the baby." I stared at Aram to gauge his response after I spoke. His expression didn't alter one bit. His eyes remained fixed on mine. "Did you hear me?" I asked.

"Yes, I heard you."

"Does it mean anything to you? Do you feel anything?"

"Kiley, were you really pregnant?" I felt my stomach drop.

"Yes, how could you think otherwise?" I could never tell him the truth.

"I had to ask. I'm not trying to be insensitive, but the whole thing just felt weird. I don't know how to explain it."

"I've had to go through all of this by myself," I said.

"I know, and I'm sorry. I feel horrible about that."

"I don't want you to feel bad. I want you to stay. I want you to give me another chance."

"I don't know, Kiley. I don't think that's a good idea."

"Why not? God, you're the only person I want to be with. You're the only person I could ever have feelings for. You're my love." My voice sounded frantic, which is exactly the way I intended it to sound.

"I don't know what to say."

"Say you can't stop thinking about me. Say you want to take me right here and now. Tell me you love me like I love you. Am I the only one who has these feelings?" Aram didn't answer. "Aram, I lost our child. Don't act like you don't care."

"I care," he said.

"Then act like it. I don't know why you keep your feelings hidden from view. Why can't you just tell me how you feel? Why can't you be there for me when I need you the most?"

"It's hard for me to feel anymore."

"Why?"

"It's easier not to."

"Aram, you can't mean that."

"Listen, I am sorry that you had to go through all of this by yourself. I don't have an answer. Sometimes we're great together. Other times I feel like we should have never been in a relationship."

"How can you say that?"

"Because sometimes it seems like all we do is fight."

"What do you want?"

"I don't know. What do you want?"

"I want you," I said. "What do you want?"

"I need to go soon," he said.

"No, don't leave me again. I want you to come back home."

"Not now, Kiley. I can't."

"I need you."

"We need some time apart."

"That makes no sense. I love you. I don't want there to be any space between us."

"There will always be space between us."

"You make me feel like shit sometimes. Do you know that?"

"I'm   sorry."

"Are you?" I asked. He didn't respond. "Damn it, Aram. Don't ignore me."

"I'm not ignoring you."

"Come here." I walked over to him and grabbed him by the hand. He didn't move. "Come here," I repeated.

"What are you doing?" he asked.

"I want you. I want to feel you inside me. I want to taste you," I said in a low voice.

"Kiley, stop."

"Aram, let me please you."

"I can't right now," he said.

"Come on. Are you afraid you'll be forced to feel something for me?" I knelt in front of Aram as I spoke. Once I was on my knees I looked up at him. I felt his hand let go of mine.

"I need to go," he said.

CHAPTER 52
DINNER WITH WILLIAM

Ashley Morrison

"How are you feeling?" William asked from across the table at the Bistro downtown. I quit staring at the neon light above the bar and looked at him before I responded.

"I'm feeling better," I said.

"That's good."

"Yeah, the new antidepressant my doctor prescribed must be working. I don't feel as negative."

"That's wonderful. You haven't been yourself lately."

"I know. I apologize. But I'm back," I chuckled. William laughed.

"All of this is great news to me!" I smiled at William and he smiled back. He reached across the table and squeezed my hand. He really did care about me.

Sad music played in the background as William told me about his day. It wasn't that I was trying to be rude, but I couldn't focus. I hadn't thought about Aram too much. I surmised that he was busy because he hadn't tried to contact me in over a week. It was better that way. The whole notion of us getting together and leaving the city was sheer nonsense. We weren't fools in love any longer.

"What are you doing next weekend?" William asked.

"I don't know. I haven't thought that far ahead."

"Shana and Annie want to take you out next weekend if you're free. They said you need a girls' night." I could hardly conceal my chagrin. I hated William's cousin, Shana. Annie was William's sister, and she wasn't much better. They were so fucking fake. I felt disgusted whenever I was forced to hang out with them. All they did was gossip about the other girls they knew. I'm sure they talked about me when I wasn't around. I didn't care.

"I don't think I have any plans," I admitted.

"Great. I'll let Annie know. She'll be excited."

"A girls' night might be just what I need," I said, half-joking.

"I agree," William replied, not picking up on my sarcasm. I took a drink of wine.

I felt William looking at me as I ate my salad. I looked up from my plate. "What?" I asked.

"Nothing," he said. He smiled and looked away.

"Tell me," I demanded.

"I'm glad you're back to yourself," he said.

"I've always been here."

"I know. But it was hard to tell at times."

"I don't know why I get that way."

"There's no reason to get so sad," William said.

"I guess you're right. I shouldn't take life so seriously. Nobody else does."

"I wouldn't go that far."

"I'm kidding," I said, even though I wasn't.

"You had everyone scared."

"Apparently so. Why was everyone freaking out?"

"Because you were acting strangely. It's probably difficult for you to see it, but we were afraid you were going to do something impulsive."

"Like what?" I asked.

"I don't know," he said.

"Like back out of the wedding?"

"Yeah, I guess I thought you might."

"I'm not backing out of the wedding. I wouldn't do that to you," I assured.

"That makes me feel better. It's just that… Oh, never mind. It doesn't matter. I'm just happy you're back."

"I'm happy that you're happy," I said.

"Good. Everyone is happy then." William laughed while looking at me.

"Could you do me a favor, though?" I asked.

"Sure, anything."

"Could you not worry my mother? You know she's crazy enough without you telling her that I'm depressed."

"I didn't tell her you were depressed."

"I know, you told her you thought I was considering not going through with the wedding. She then assumed I was suffering from some mental breakdown. I think she was ready to have me committed. Please, don't tell her anything she might use against me. She lost it and made me feel like shit."

"I didn't know," he said.

"Of course. She would never tell you anything. She waits and waits until she has the opportunity to attack me and then she makes me feel like I'm an inch tall."

"What did she say?"

"A bunch of stupid shit about me ruining my life and about how I need to grow up. It's always the same bullshit speech from her. The basic summary is I'm a loser and need to transition into a more mature mindset if I ever want to make anything out of my life."

"Jesus, she said that?"

"In so many words, yes. She's fucking insane. I think she resents me for some reason."

"That's odd."

"Yes it is. Can you please watch what you tell her though? I don't want to deal with her freaking out again. I don't know if I can take it."

"Sure. I'm so sorry. I didn't know she said those things to you. That makes me feel terrible. I was worried about you and didn't know who to talk to about it. I wanted to help."

"Don't worry about me, William. I'll be fine."

"I love you. I can't stop worrying about you."

"I love you too." I said. I was pretty sure I did love William. I knew he cared deeply for me. There was no reason not to love him. I took another drink of wine and felt the exhilarating warmth settle in my stomach.

"We're going to make it through this wedding, Ash. I promise you."

"I sure hope so," I joked.

"We will. I know it's been stressing you out lately. But next week marks the beginning of July. Can you believe it? We're three weeks away from being husband and wife."

"I can't wait," I said.

"Me either. I've waited for quite a while to call you mine. In three weeks, it will be official."

"I'm yours." I looked directly at William as I spoke.

"I believe you," he said. I couldn't help everything that had happened with Aram. Aram didn't love me though. He loved the old me, the one he used to know. He didn't know me and I didn't know him any longer. I vowed right there while sitting across from William at dinner that I would let go of the remnants of my past in order to create a future with William. I didn't want to tell Aram, but I had to. I couldn't lie to William anymore. As I considered the past few months, I didn't feel any guilt. I couldn't. After all, life is only a small glimpse into the abounding nothingness, and while it may be impossible to ever truly know anyone, I think I'll still try.

CHAPTER 53
IS IT OVER?

Turner Brennan

It was after one in the afternoon and Aram and I were still in bed. My body felt tingly. He had made love to me twice, and although his kisses on my back felt so good, I wasn't sure my body could handle a third time. I had planned to tell him about my pregnancy that afternoon, but I couldn't escape my pleasure. I didn't want to ruin it.

I heard Aram shifting in bed. "Do you want something to drink? I'm going to get a water," he said as he got out of bed.

"I'll take one too, if you don't mine."

"Coming right up." I turned over and watched him as he walked to the kitchen. I loved how he walked. My legs were still shaking.

"I need to talk to you about something," Aram yelled from the kitchen. I could hear him digging around in the refrigerator for the bottles of water.

"What's on your mind?" I asked. I covered my legs with the sheet so he wouldn't see me still shaking.

"Just a second," he said as he closed the refrigerator. I twirled my hair with my finger as I watched him emerge from the kitchen. He smiled as he approached the bed. I still couldn't believe he was with me. He handed me a bottle of water and then opened his own. I sat up in bed.

"Kiley isn't doing well," Aram blurted after he took a drink. I didn't bother opening my bottle.

"What?" I asked, unsure if I heard him correctly.

"Kiley. She's not doing well at all," he repeated.

"Okay. What am I supposed to say?"

"Nothing."

"Well…I hope she starts doing better soon." I think it was obvious to Aram that I didn't really care.

"I don't know what to do to help her," he said.

"Why do you have to do anything? She's not your concern any longer," I said.

"You don't understand."

"What don't I understand?"

"I've never seen her like this. I think something might happen."

"What do you mean?" I asked, feeling more annoyed as the conversation progressed.

"I think she might harm herself or something. I don't know. I didn't think she'd ever be this bad. She's kind of lost it."

"Are you fucking serious, Aram?" I couldn't refrain from saying it.

"Yes."

"No, I mean you don't see what she's doing?"

"What are you talking about?"

"This is all a ploy. She's playing you. Don't you see it?"

"I don't think she is. She's miserable."

"Of course she's miserable. She's probably heartbroken, but that doesn't mean she's going to harm herself. It's a ruse to get you back."

"How so?"

"Because if you feel sorry for her, you might come back to her. She wants you back; it's so apparent."

"You don't know the full story," he retorted.

"I know she's crazy. She wants to control you. Why can't you see that?"

"Turner, I wish you wouldn't say that."

"Don't tell me you believe her."

"I didn't want to tell you..." Aram began before I interrupted.

"Tell me what?"

"She was pregnant."

"What do you mean, she *was* pregnant?"

"She had a miscarriage."

"Jesus, are you serious?"

"Yes."

"She's fucking lying, Aram. Can't you see through her bullshit? That's all it is— bullshit and lies."

"I don't think so. I don't know."

"Trust me, it is. You would know if she was pregnant."

"Think so?"

"Yes. Don't believe her. She's a fucking liar."

"I don't know what to believe."

"She can tell you anything she wants. That doesn't mean that she's telling you the truth."

"I don't want her to harm herself."

"Do you think she really would?"

"I think it's possible."

"She's got you then," I said. "She's going to get you back."

"I don't want to be with her," he said.

"It doesn't matter."

"Why do you say that?"

"Because sometimes people end up with someone they shouldn't be with. It's just the way it happens," I said. I felt sick. I couldn't catch my breath.

"I can't just leave her to suffer by herself."

"Why not?" I asked. "I don't understand why you believe her. I don't understand any of this."

"I just need some time. I need to figure out how to make this easier for her," he said. He was still holding his water, even though he hadn't taken a drink in a while.

"What about me, Aram?" I asked. I couldn't look at him any longer.

"You know how I feel about you. I'll be back."

"I don't know how you feel about me because you never tell me. I'd do anything for you, don't you know that? I want to be with you."

"You are with me," he said.

"What should I do?"

"Wait on me."

"What if I can't?" I asked.

"I don't know. I guess you have to do what's best for you."

"You're what's best for me. I wish you could see that."

"I do. Damn."

"I have a bad feeling about this, Aram."

"Why?"

"I don't think you'll ever be back. It feels like I'm losing you."

"I promise you're not."

"Promises don't mean anything," I said.

"I have to help her if I can."

"Then go! Go help Kiley."

"Please don't be like this," he said in a soft voice.

"Aram, I'm not going to act like this isn't killing me. I can't. I refuse to act like I don't care."

"I'm sorry," he said.

"Don't say that. Don't say anything else. Just come back to me. I don't want to hear any more explanations or justifications. I don't want you to apologize. I want you to do what you feel you have to do, and then come back to me. That's what I want."

"I'll come back to you," he said.

"She's lying to you."

"You may be right."

"I know I am."

CHAPTER 54
ARAM'S RETURN

Kiley Adams

It all happened so quickly. Aram knocked on my door after I was already in bed. I answered the door and he walked inside my apartment without saying a word. I tried to speak, but he told me not to. He led me to the bedroom and cornered me against the wall. Before I could even process what was happening, his lips were pressed against mine and I felt his tongue in my mouth. All I could do was respond by kissing him back as my heart raced in my chest. His hand touched my inner thigh. I could feel his breath on my neck. I thought it all was a dream as our shadows became one. After it was over I whispered, "I love you," to him, but he didn't say anything.

The next morning I awoke early and made some coffee. I knew Aram would sleep late. I couldn't help but wonder where he had been and what he had done. *Why had he returned?* None of that mattered as I watched him sleeping. I stood in the doorway of the bedroom and drank my coffee. His breaths were slow and deep. I loved the way his muscles always appeared to be flexed. I could still taste him as I traced my lips with my forefinger. I took another drink from my coffee.

Aram turned over in bed to find me watching him sleep. I felt embarrassed, but he didn't appear to mind.

"What are you doing, Kiley?" he asked while rubbing his eyes with his palms.

"Nothing," I said. There was an awkward pause as Aram sat up in bed. "I made some coffee. Would you like a cup?"

"Sure."

I handed Aram his coffee and sat beside him in bed. We both leaned against the headboard and looked at the single beam of sunlight shining through the window. Just then the air conditioner kicked on.

"It's going to be another hot one, isn't it," Aram commented.

"I couldn't believe it was you last night. You surprised me," I said.

"Did it upset you?"

"How could it?"

"I'm just making sure that this is OK. I don't know what has happened or what will happen in the future. All I do know is that I felt the need to see you last night."

"I'm glad you did," I said while smiling. I reached over and hugged Aram.

"Easy," he said as he shielded his mug of coffee.

"I can't believe it. It's you!" I exclaimed. I hugged him again.

"Kiley, you're going to make me spill this coffee."

"I don't care," I said.

"You will when it scalds you!"

"Nonsense. Nothing could damper my mood." I leaned in and kissed his cheek and then his lips.

Aram sat his mug on the floor and looked at me.

"What?" I asked.

"What are you doing today?"

"I'm not sure. What are your plans?"

"I don't think I have any."

"Let's go somewhere," I said excitedly.

"Where?"

"I don't care. Let's go, though. I don't want to be here today."

"Why not?" he asked.

"I feel like we're starting over."

"Maybe we are."

"Let's take a train somewhere. Doesn't that sound fun?"

"I have to work tomorrow," he said.

"Well, shit. How about we take a long walk downtown? We could grab a late lunch or something."

"That would work."

"Did you miss me when you were gone?" I had to ask.

"Kiley..."

"I'll understand if you didn't. I know you were pretty mad at me."

"It's not that," he said. I was confused.

"What was it then?"

"I don't know. It's just a lot has happened."

"Like what?" I persisted.

"I don't feel like any of this is real. Maybe it never was real."

"What are you talking about?" Aram was losing me.

"You never feel as though life doesn't have any meaning? It's disturbing."

"Is life supposed to mean something?"

"I don't think so any longer. I used to believe it did. I used to think that everything happens for a reason and that everything works out for the better in the end."

"Why don't you believe that anymore?"

"I don't know."

"There has to be a reason," I said.

"I think it's loving and not being loved that caused me to lose faith." I didn't know how to respond to Aram's statement. He stared straight ahead as he spoke. I felt powerless to help him. I caressed the backside of his hand. He didn't respond.

"The worst part is..." Aram began again before he abruptly stopped.

"What is the worst part?" I asked him. I squeezed his hand in mine.

"I'm going to take a shower," he said after a long pause.

"OK…" I said, feeling bewildered. Aram moved the sheet and got out of bed. His naked body looked even better in the light. As he walked out of the room and shut the bathroom door, I thought of the past year with him. I heard the shower start and imagined how he looked with water running down his body. I would never know Aram. I could only know pieces of him.

CHAPTER 55
I CAN'T LEAVE

Ashley Morrison

I met Aram near the bus station. As I approached him, he smiled and started walking toward me. He hugged me before I could say anything. I hugged him back, although it only made what I had to say more difficult. He felt good. I could never forget how he smelled. I had to tell him it was over.

"I'm starting to lose it, Ash. When are we leaving?"

"What?" I asked.

"Don't give me that. You know what I'm talking about. I haven't heard from you in nearly two weeks. Have you figured out how you're going to do it?"

"Do what?"

"Leave William."

"Aram..." I began before he stopped me.

"Don't fucking tell me you're backing out of this. Don't say it, Ashley. I won't let you give up on us," he said with such passion that I didn't respond immediately.

"Aram, it's not as easy as you make it sound," I eventually remarked.

"I never said it was easy. None of this has been easy."

"I'm not leaving," I said bluntly.

"Goddamn it, Ashley. Did your mother talk to you or something?"

"What? No!"

"Jesus, she did, didn't she. You're fucking twenty-eight years old. You don't have to please her. You have to please yourself. This is your life."

"I know."

"Do you?"

I couldn't take Aram yelling at me. I already felt half-dead inside. I couldn't allow the last bit of life I had remaining inside me to be suffocated. I started walking away from the station. I heard him say something and then he followed me.

"Ash. Ash!" he yelled as he walked behind me.

"I can't do this, Aram. I just can't." My voice cracked. I could feel tears coming. "It's over."

"No it's not," he said.

"I'm going to marry William."

"You don't have to do that. We've talked about this. That's fucking insane. You love me."

"I love him," I said.

"No you don't. You don't love him like you love me. You can't."

"It's different, Aram."

"It's different because what you feel for him isn't love. You know that. You told me that last time we talked. What happened to you since then?"

"I don't know."

"I don't know what to do, Ash. I want you. I want us to be to-gether. We have to be together. You're the person I'm supposed to be with."

"Says who?"

"Says me. Says my stomach that won't stop twisting. Says my heart that won't stop racing when you're around. Don't you feel the same way?"

"Aram, there is no destiny here. We had some good times. It's over, though. I'm sorry if I led you on in any way. I've been confused."

"You sound like you are still confused."

"Probably," I said.

"Don't be the victim, Ashley. Don't."

"Aren't we all victims?" I asked between sobs. I felt so much hurt that I was sure I would never fully heal. A gust of wind pushed my hair off my shoulders and provided a brief reprieve from the heat. Aram grabbed me by the arms and pulled me near.

"Look at me, Ash. Unless you take control of your life, you're going to be marrying someone else in less than three weeks. Do you know that? You can't postpone dealing with this any longer. The time to act is now. You have to do something."

"I know," I said. I felt so fatigued I didn't think I had the strength to break free from Aram. He leaned in and tried to kiss me. I turned away so that he couldn't, though his hands still held onto my arms.

"I can't keep doing this," he said after he failed to kiss me. "I can't! This is slowly killing me. *You're* slowly killing me! Do you know that?"

"I can't be with you, Aram."

"Why the fuck not?" he shouted.

"Because. We tried it and it didn't work."

"You're willing to quit on us and everything we had? You're going to marry William and act as though all of this never happened?"

"I could never do that."

"Then I don't understand."

"I don't either."

"You're not making any sense," he complained.

"I know. I don't understand any of this enough to articulate it any better. All I know is that I can't be with you."

"How do you know that and nothing else?"

"It's what I have to do."

"It's what you think you have to do. There's a difference. Can't you see how much you hurt me?"

"I know," I answered.

"Do you? Because you don't act like you give a shit either way."

233

"I do care," I screamed. A few people looked at us as if they were attempting to discern whether or not I needed assistance. I broke from Aram at that moment, but I couldn't walk away from him. They stopped looking at us once they realized I was crying. People don't like to watch others cry. It's unbecoming. It's easier to turn away.

"So what do I do?" Aram asked while staring at me. I couldn't tell if it was pain or hate in his eyes. I surmised it was probably a bit of both.

"Move on with your life."

"And how in the fuck am I supposed to do that? How am I supposed to leave today and know I'll never see the girl I love again? How is that supposed to ever be okay? How can I ever be expected to heal from that?"

"I don't have any answers, Aram. I know time helps, but I don't know if people ever fully recover from love."

"This is all so fucking ugly. I hate this feeling. You can't leave," he pleaded. I didn't respond. He looked at me and then looked away. I noticed tears forming in his eyes. I only remember seeing tears in his eyes once before and that was when his father had a heart attack. Later that same evening I held him in bed and felt a few tears hit my arm. He never mentioned anything to me about that night. He didn't have to.

"Everything will be okay," I said. I didn't know what to say. I wanted to console him but everything I thought of sounded artificial and useless.

"Don't say that, Ashley. You don't know that everything is going to be fine. You don't know anything."

"You're probably right. I do know I never meant to hurt you."

"Does that matter? It's irrelevant whether you intended to hurt me or not. I'm hurt. That's my reality. Now you're telling me that you're going to marry another man and I'm supposed to accept it and act like everything between us never happened."

"I hope you never forget us," I blurted.

"So this is it? Are you sure, Ashley?"

"I'm sorry," I said.

"No you're not! Quit saying shit you don't mean." There was a pause before Aram erupted. "Just go. Go to your home. Go be with your soon-to-be husband."

"Aram, I am sorry. I mean it."

"You don't mean anything you say."

CHAPTER 56
PARK SWINGS

Turner Brennan

I felt the wind rush through my hair as my stomach turned. I couldn't remember the last time I enjoyed the park swings. I used to love them when I was a little girl. They made me feel like I could fly. I loved believing I could go anywhere and do anything. I closed my eyes and felt the back and forth motions erase all my troubles for a few precious moments. I wished I could always feel that same serenity.

I allowed the bottoms of my shoes to drag against the dirt until I had stopped swinging. Alaina, my good friend from high school, had agreed to meet me. I didn't know who to talk to about Aram and about my pregnancy. I felt alone.

"I haven't been here in a long while," Alaina said. "Remember when we used to come here on the weekends and talk about boys? Those were such carefree days."

"Those days were the best. How have you been?" I asked. I gripped the chains holding the swing.

"My life is boring. I'm still living at home and working at the bar. I want to start taking classes in the fall, but I don't know. I'm not sure what I want to do. I don't really want to do anything. I hate growing up."

"I agree."

"What about you, Turner? I haven't heard from you since summer hit. When was the last time we hung out? Wasn't it during your spring break?" she asked.

"Yes, I believe so. That's crazy."

"I know. So what's new with you?"

"Everything," I said in a solemn tone.

"Are you okay?"

"I don't know. Not really."

"What's wrong?" Alaina sat on the swing next to me.

"I don't know what to do."

"What do you mean?"

"I'm pregnant," I said. There was a long pause. I looked down at my shoes as I dug my foot into the dirt underneath the swing. I could hear the chains holding the swing creaking with my movements.

"Who is the father?" Alaina finally asked.

"I'm really not sure."

"Oh…" Alaina became obviously uncomfortable.

"I think I know who it is."

"That's good."

"The worst part is I think I've lost the person I love," I continued.

"Really? I didn't know you were seeing anyone."

"It's Aram."

"The older guy you've had a crush on for years?" she asked.

"Yes. We finally started hanging out."

"That's amazing."

"It was even better than I imagined it would be. He actually lived with me for a while."

"Damn, Turner. That's crazy. I had no idea. Wasn't he living with some girl?"

"Yes, but they broke up. Well, they broke up for a while."

"Are they together again?"

"I'm not sure. I don't even know why he left. He said he was worried about her."

"The other girl?"

"Yes."

"But you're pregnant," she said.

"He doesn't know."

"He doesn't know you're pregnant? You didn't tell him?"

"No. I couldn't."

"Why not? Don't you think you should?"

"I don't know. I'm so confused. I love him."

"Then you have to tell him, Turner. He would want to know."

"Do you think so?"

"Absolutely."

"I guess I'm afraid."

"Afraid of what?" she asked.

"I don't know what I would do if I knew he didn't want to be with me. I don't know how I would respond. I can't imagine my life without him."

"Do you think it's over?"

"I have no idea. I try not to think about it," I said.

"Are you going to have the baby?"

"Yes."

"Who else could be the father?"

"A guy who I met in the art store named Jakob."

"Does he know you're pregnant?"

"No. I quit talking to him."

"Why?"

"Because I started seeing Aram. Jakob still calls, but I quit responding."

"What if he is the father instead of Aram?"

"I don't know. Jakob is a great guy. I mean, he's perfect. He's nice, intelligent, handsome, and artistic."

"Then why aren't you with him?" Alaina asked.

"Because he's not Aram."

"Did Aram pass the test?"

"What test?" I replied.

"The test... When Aram talks to you, when he touches you, do you find it difficult to breathe? That's the test. That's when you know it's real love," she said.

"Yes, that's exactly how he makes me feel."

"Then you need to go after him. Don't let him go without a fight," she said.

"I don't intend to let him go. But it's not easy. None of this is easy. All I can think about is what happens if he is back with Kiley for good. I don't know what I would do. I can't think of him with another. It kills me to imagine him holding someone else."

"I wish I had an answer for you, Turner."

"That's not why I wanted to meet you," I said. "I needed to talk to someone about all of this. I haven't told anyone."

"Is there anything I can do, Turner? Anything at all?"

"Yes," I said.

"What can I do?"

"Will you stay with me? Just for a little while longer."

"Sure."

"I don't want to be alone right now."

CHAPTER 57
GIRLS' NIGHT OUT

Ashley Morrison

The summer air felt heavy. I had already been to two bars with Annie and Shana. The following week was it. I would be married then. I couldn't think of myself as a wife. I had trouble imagining it changing me in any way. I didn't want to think about it.

"It's right across the street," Annie said as we walked along the sidewalk. I didn't care where we went. All I wanted to do was get drunk. Annie wanted to meet up with some of her friends. Shana kept bumping into me on accident. She complained her heels were the issue. I wanted to ditch both of them.

I left Annie and Shana at the table and made my way to the bar. I told them I was getting a drink, but I really wanted to leave them behind because they annoyed me so much. I couldn't stand them.

"What would you like?" the bartender yelled over the noise of the bar.

"Whiskey and Coke," I replied. I sat on a stool. I took my cell phone out of my pocket and started to text William but then stopped. A group of guys stood behind me. I could hear them talking about my ass. All guys are the same. They all become animals when they drink.

I turned around to find Annie's friends seated at the table. I decided to stay away as long as possible.

A guy from the group behind me sat on the stool beside me and leaned into me.

"You're beautiful," he said. I looked at him. I didn't say anything. I then looked back to my drink. I stirred it with the little red straw and then took a drink. I could feel the guy's eyes looking at me, expecting me to respond in some way. I refused to.

"Whatever, bitch," he finally said. I smiled to myself and took another drink. They're all the same.

I finished my Whiskey and Coke and ordered a second. The group of guys left. Once my second drink arrived, I returned to the table.

"Where have you been?" Annie asked.

"Drinking." I replied. They laughed. I didn't.

"Ashley, this is Julie and Terra." Annie took a sip from her drink after introducing me to her friends.

"Nice to meet you," I said. They smiled.

"So, how does it feel?" Terra asked.

"How does what feel?" I responded.

"To almost be married. You must be excited."

"Yeah, it's crazy," I said.

"I can't imagine."

I staggered a bit when I arose from my seat to approach the bar for another drink. My vision was blurry, but I felt good. I parted my way through the crowd until I was standing next to the bar. As I waited, I felt my phone vibrating in the front pocket of my jeans. I pulled it out to see who had sent me a text. It was from William. It said, "I love you." I stared at it for a moment and then I turned my phone off without responding.

"What can I get you?" the bartender yelled.

"Another Whiskey and Coke," I said.

"Coming right up." I leaned against the bar in order to avoid appearing drunk. I turned and watched the people talking to one another. *Did anyone else ever have the thoughts I have?*

I made my way back to the table after getting my drink.

"Are you okay?" Shana asked once I sat down.

"Yes, why?" I said.

"I saw you almost trip back there." Everyone laughed.

"I'm doing just fine," I confirmed. "Aren't we here to have a good time?"

"Of course," Annie interjected.

"Well OK, then."

"What's does your dress look like?" Terra asked.

"It's white." I replied.

"Ha-ha. Do you have a picture?"

"Nope," I lied. Of course I had a picture on my phone. But I didn't want to show them because I didn't want to look at it.

"Oh," she said, as if she was seriously disappointed.

"It's beautiful," Annie commented. "William sent me some pictures of it."

"Where did you find it?" Julie asked. I didn't understand everyone's preoccupation with the stupid dress.

"I forget. I was with my mother. The process felt more like torture than anything." Everyone laughed after I spoke.

"What color are your flowers?" Shana asked.

"Yellow, I think."

"They're going to France for their honeymoon," Annie said.

"That would be so romantic," Shana added.

"It should be pleasant," I said.

"You're a lucky girl," Terra proclaimed.

All the girls had since made their way to the dance floor and were dancing while I stayed at the table drinking. I couldn't remember how many drinks I had, but after taking two shots of Patrón, I couldn't feel much.

"How are you tonight?" I heard a voice ask. I turned to see a young guy sitting at the table.

"Who are you?" I asked, without thinking.

He chuckled. "I'm Kyle. Who are you?" He extended his hand. I shook it.

"I'm Ashley." I took a drink from my Whiskey and Coke. I kept blinking to steady my vision.

"Are you here with anyone?" he asked.

"Well…not really," I replied. "I'm supposed to be hanging out with those girls," I said while pointing toward Annie and Shana who were both dancing like sluts with two guys.

"Oh, but you're not having fun?"

"I don't really like them." My words slurred together.

"I see. Would you like another drink?" he asked.

"I can get my own."

"I'm not trying to come across as forward. You look interesting," he said.

"I'm not interesting."

"What makes you say that?"

"Before we continue this charade, I should tell you something," I said.

"What's that?"

"I hate men."

"Why?"

"Do I need a reason?" I asked.

* * *

Apparently I blacked out. I don't remember going to the bathroom, but when I came to, I was sitting next to the toilet in one of the stalls with vomit all over the toilet seat.

"Ashley, let me in," Annie said. I didn't say anything. I wanted to be alone. She knocked again. "Ashley. You have to unlock the door so I can get in."

I awoke to Annie and Shana leading me into my house. I heard William asking what happened to me.

"She had too much to drink," Annie said in a somber tone.

"What all did she have?" William asked.

"I don't know. She's been throwing up though. You will want to watch her."

They led me into the bathroom. Annie stayed with me while Shana retrieved some towels.

"Are you feeling okay, honey?" Annie asked.

"I feel great," I replied. I lifted the lid of the toilet and vomited again.

"You don't look great," William said.

"Then don't look at me," I said while gasping for breath. I wiped my mouth with my forearm.

"I'll go get her some water," he said.

"You're going to be fine," Shana said as she wetted the towel in her hand. She gave it to me and I wiped my mouth with it.

"I want to be alone," I said.

"I don't think that's a good idea," Annie said.

"I want to be alone," I repeated.

CHAPTER 58

THIS IS REAL

Kiley Adams

Aram hadn't said a word for over an hour. He sat silently in the passenger seat and messed with the radio while I drove. I had convinced him to take a trip to Chicago. He said he wanted to be away for the weekend. I wasn't sure why, but I figured he wanted us to have an opportunity to get to know each other again. Everything had been different since he returned. The forecast called for rain the entire weekend. I could see dark clouds in the distance. I figured we would get a hotel room downtown and then go to the art museum. I never cared for art, but I knew Aram liked looking at the paintings. It didn't matter to me, as long as I was with Aram.

Big rain drops dotted the windshield. I turned the wipers on and then shut them off. The sun was still visible, but I could tell the rain was coming.

"What are you thinking about?" I finally asked Aram.

"Nothing," he said.

"You have to be thinking about something."

"It's not important."

"What is it?"

"I'd rather not talk about it." I turned the wipers on and off again to clear away the raindrops that had just fallen. Aram quit messing with the radio. He reclined his seat and stared out the passenger window.

"Are you hungry?" I asked.

"Not really. Are you?"

"Not really," I replied. I was desperate for conversation. I hate silence. There's something so lonely about it. "Do you still want to go to the art museum tomorrow?"

"Sure."

"Is there any exhibit you want to visit?" I could feel myself growing nervous.

"No," he said flatly.

"What's wrong, Aram?"

"Nothing is wrong. Why do you keep asking me questions?"

"Something is wrong. I can tell. You're being distant."

"I'm a distant person."

"No you're not. You can be engaging when you want to be. You haven't been yourself since we got back together. I'm putting all of me in this relationship. I want us to work. I want it so badly, Aram. Do you believe me?"

"I have no reason not to."

"Why are you acting like you don't care? I know you do. You have to care; otherwise you wouldn't have come back to me. You returned for a reason. There's a part of us that knows that this relationship will work. I know it won't be easy. Nothing worthwhile is. I want it to work, though." There was a pause. I wasn't certain, but I suspected Aram was provoking me. I didn't understand why.

"Can you say something, please?" I asked.

"What do you want me to say?" he asked. He was still staring out the window instead of looking at me.

"You could begin by looking at me when you talk to me." Aram turned his head deliberately. He appeared resentful. "Talk to me, baby. I love you."

"Can you stop at the next exit?" he asked.

"Why?"

"So I can get something to drink. I'm thirsty."

"Are you serious?"

"Yes. Why would I lie about that?"

"I don't know. It's just a random request when I'm trying to have a serious conversation with you."

"I can't help being thirsty, Kiley. Let's not make every little situation an ordeal. I don't have the energy to deal with that." I couldn't believe him. It was as though he hadn't heard a word I had said about our relationship.

"I'll take the next exit for you," I said.

"Thank you." He then turned his head again so he could look out his window.

"I'm glad we're taking this trip," I revealed to Aram soon after.

"Me too," he said.

"Really? Are you really glad?"

"I said I was, didn't I?"

"It's just that you haven't been very easy to understand lately."

"Was I ever?"

"Well, not really. But lately, it's impossible to know what you're thinking or feeling."

"I don't know what is real any longer," he said.

"Why do you say that?"

"Because it's true."

"What do you mean?"

"I don't know where I belong."

"You belong right here," I said. I looked away from the road to see Aram's reaction. His expression didn't alter. "Aram, look at me," I commanded. Aram didn't respond at first, but then he turned his head to face me. "This is real. I am real. Love is real," I said.

"How are you so sure?" he asked.

"I just am." There was another pause. Aram turned his head to look out his window again. "Can you ever love me?" I asked.

"I can try."

CHAPTER 59
HOMECOMING

Turner Brennan

My mother sat across the table from me in the kitchen. She stopped for a second and stared at me in disbelief. I didn't know what to do. I felt ashamed.

"What are you going to do?" she asked as her stare became more and more distant.

"I don't know," I responded. I had just told her everything. I told her about Jakob. I told her about Aram. I told her how they were both gone now and I told her about how I didn't know how I would ever smile again without Aram in my life.

"Is Aram the father? Have you talked to either one of them?"

"Does it matter?" I don't know why I felt the need to be defiant. I guess I felt inferior for some reason.

"Turner, have you talked to either one of them?"

"No." I looked out the big window in the kitchen. A sparrow perched on the windowsill and then flew away.

"Why not?" my mother asked.

"He doesn't want me," I said.

"Turner, you've got to stop this."

"Stop what?" I asked in a louder voice.

"You're not a little girl. You don't have time to pout. You need to figure out who the father of this child is. You need to act like an adult. This is just the beginning. The child will need a father and you will need support. Don't you think for a second that your father and I are supporting this child while you finish school. This is your predicament. If you choose to have this child, you will be its mother. We'll help you, of course, but you will be the parent."

"I know this, mother."

"Then I shouldn't have to tell you this," she continued. "Do you have an idea of which one is the father?"

"I think it's Aram. I want it to be Aram."

"God, Turner. What has Aram done for you? He left you, right?"

"I love him, mom. I'm in love with him. I can't help that." She didn't know what to say to that. She looked away. I could tell she was disgusted. I wished that she could meet Aram. She would see why I loved him so much. *Why did he leave me?*

My mother got up from her seat and walked away. I thought she was done talking to me. I almost started to cry.

"Do you want some tea?" she asked.

"Yes, please," I replied. I could hear her pouring the tea into the kettle and switching the stove on. I could hear the cupboards open and close and the sound of two mugs being placed on the counter. I wanted to hug her. I wanted to hug someone and feel them hug me back. I had always felt isolated. I thought I would get used to it at some point, but I never did. Loneliness was an expansive chasm that always reminded me I'm not pretty enough, smart enough, or good enough for anyone to truly love me. My life could accurately be described as a perpetual search to find someone or something to offset the emptiness. There remained a lingering possibility that I could eventually be made whole, though realistically I knew that was unlikely. No matter what, everyone clings to hope. It's humanity's greatest flaw.

My mother walked back to the table and handed me a mug of warm tea. I felt the warmth of the mug against my palms. I looked out the window and noticed the sky was getting darker.

"Is it supposed to rain today?" I asked before taking a sip of tea.

"Yeah. It's supposed to be nasty all weekend," she said. We sat across from one another without saying anything for a long time. We both stared out the window at something that wasn't there.

"You know I love you, right? I mean, I have always loved you, Turner. Nothing could ever change that. You're my child."

"I know." I never doubted it, but it felt good to hear her say it.

"You'll feel the same way about your child." I wanted to cry. I wasn't sure why. "I'm sorry if I sounded upset. The news caught me off guard. I didn't mean for it to sound as if I wouldn't support you."

"I know, mom."

"You need to contact Jakob and Aram. That's the right thing to do. They need to be involved."

"I guess you're right," I conceded.

"You'll also need to get a paternity test."

"I don't want to think about that."

"Turner, you have to do it. If not for you, then for your child," she said in a sincere tone.

"I know I need to. I just don't want to think about it at the moment. I don't know how all of this happened. I mean, everything was going great with Aram."

"Why did he leave?" she asked.

"His ex-girlfriend was suicidal or something. I don't know. I think it was all a scam to get him to feel bad and come back to her."

"It sounds like it."

"I don't know how he could leave. I just don't! Didn't he feel what I felt?"

"I can't answer that."

"This all is so tough." I felt like I was going to start crying uncontrollably.

"Turner, it's okay to feel strongly about someone."

"I can't do it again. I can't allow myself to."

"It feels that way now, but you will again someday. And when you find the right person, you'll be glad you did."

"I don't want to be with anyone besides Aram. He's the one I will always love."

"You may always love him. That's true. But you'll move on." I could see the concern on my mom's face. I looked away and stared out the window again to avoid crying. A few large raindrops hit the glass and then it started to downpour. I knew I would forever be haunted by what never was. Somehow, I would have to learn how to smile again.

CHAPTER 60
WEDDING

Ashley Morrison

I wanted to hear his voice. I had to hear it. I needed to feel the exhilaration one last time. It had been raining all day. I knew he would call. He had to. I craved him in every single way. If I heard his voice years from now, would I still find it difficult to breathe? Would my chest still burn when I thought of him? Would I feel lightheaded at the thought of his touch? Only Aram had the power to save me from myself. *Why hadn't he called yet?*

"I absolutely love this dress," my mother said as she entered the room while cradling my dress in her arms. I didn't say anything. "Don't let the rain get you down, Ashley. The ceremony will still be beautiful. The storm will give you something to remember. It provides character."

"Excuse me, do you mind if I take some pictures?" the annoying photographer said from the doorway.

"Sure," I said. She smiled and walked into the room where I was seated in front of a mirror. I could hear the camera snapping behind me. I couldn't concentrate.

"Make sure you get some pictures of the dress. Here, let's drape it over your chair, Ashley. Stand up, honey. We'll place your shoes on the seat too." I stood up and stared into the mirror as the photographer busily positioned the dress on the chair. "Ashley, where are your shoes," my mother asked. I walked out of the room.

I locked the bathroom door behind me. I felt panicked. I walked over to the sink and turned the water on. I cupped my hands and splashed some water on my face. Annie was supposed to arrive in thirty minutes to apply my makeup. I felt sick. I allowed the water to drip from my face before I dabbed it dry with a paper towel. I dug into my purse and found my package of cigarettes. I withdrew the small joint I rolled last night and lit it. I tried to blow the smoke toward the vent by the light. Everything slowed down. I took my phone from my purse and checked it. I still didn't have any missed calls. I finished the joint and flushed what remained down the toilet. I took a small bottle of perfume from my purse and squirted it toward the ceiling. I applied a few eye drops and dabbed the tears from my eyes with a paper towel. I looked at myself one last time in the mirror and then unlocked the bathroom door.

"It's terrible outside," Annie said. She was fifteen minutes late. I felt drops of water hit my legs when she closed her umbrella.

"Annie, we need to get going on Ashley's makeup," my mother directed. I could tell Annie was annoyed but was trying to disguise it. I didn't care if she was miserable. "Ashley, where is your necklace?" my mother asked. "Oh, never mind. I found it." After she located the necklace, she walked out of the room.

I watched people I hardly knew walk in and out of the room as Annie dutifully applied my makeup.

"Here she is," my mother said when she returned. Shana followed her with a bag of hair products. The humidity had nearly ruined any hope that my hair would look presentable. "Her hair is so frizzy. Can you fix it?" she asked.

"Sure. It shouldn't be a problem," Shana answered.

"You're a lifesaver," my mother said.

"It's coming along, Ash. Don't you think?" Annie asked. I nodded approval.

"Ashley, where is your bracelet?" my mother asked. I held up my arm to show her I was wearing it. "Oh good, you have it on. I was about to have a heart attack," she said in a frantic tone.

My buzz was almost gone and I felt restless. I needed a cigarette but I knew my mother would freak out because of the smell. I decided it wasn't worth the trouble.

"Do you need to stand up before we do your hair?" Shana asked. I stood up and walked over to the window. It was still dark and raining outside. I stood for a moment watching the raindrops pelt the glass. Then I walked over to my purse and checked my phone. I still didn't have any messages. I had never felt more alone.

"Are you ready to start?" Shana asked.

Once my dress was on, I looked at myself in the mirror and then turned so that I could see how it looked from the side. I looked fat in it. *Had I gained weight?*

"You look so beautiful, Ashley," my mother commented. Everyone in the room agreed with her. *Were they mocking me? I looked so fat!*

"Girls, you better get dressed. We have about forty minutes until the ceremony. Bob wants to start promptly at four," my mother said. Shana and Annie left to go change. My mother stayed with me. I sat down in the chair and looked at myself in the mirror.

"What are you thinking, Ashley?" my mother asked. I looked at her in the mirror. She was smiling.

When Shana and Annie returned, my mother left to go get ready. I don't know why, but people felt obligated to stay with me for support or something.

"You look so beautiful," Annie said as Shana ran her fingers through a few curls in the back of my head. "I'm glad we're going to be family." I didn't know what to say, so I didn't say anything. I wanted to check my phone.

"You're so lucky," Shana said.

"Why do you say that?" I asked.

"Because you have it all," she said. "You have the perfect man, the perfect house, and you're about to have the perfect wedding. I'm so jealous."

Shana's words resonated with me long after she had left with Annie to check on William and his groomsmen. As I looked in the mirror, I knew I should consider myself lucky. William is a great guy. That's what didn't make sense. Despite everything, I felt lost. When I looked at myself in the mirror, I saw a stranger. It didn't look like me. It didn't feel like me. I checked my phone. *Should I call Aram?*

It is the most important day of my life but it doesn't feel at all like I thought it would. Everyone tells me they are happy for me. I know I should be happy too. I can't help but question if anyone is really happy. Sometimes it feels as though happiness is just a word people say to hide the despair of not knowing anything. I hear music playing.

"Are you coming, Ash?" Annie whispers from the doorway.

"I'll be right there," I say. I pick up my phone again. Life is full of choices.